I SEE
REALITY

I SEE

TWELVE SHORT STORIES ABOUT REAL LIFE

REALITY

Jay Clark   Trisha Leaver

Kristin Elizabeth Clark   Kekla Magoon

Heather Demetrios   Marcella Pixley

Stephen Emond   James Preller

Patrick Flores-Scott   Jason Schmidt

Faith Erin Hicks   Jordan Sonnenblick

COMPILED BY GRACE KENDALL

FARRAR STRAUS GIROUX

NEW YORK

Farrar Straus Giroux Books for Young Readers
175 Fifth Avenue, New York 10010

Printed in the United States of America
Designed by Kristie Radwilowicz
First edition, 2016
10 9 8 7 6 5 4 3 2 1

fiercereads.com
reaLITyreads.com

Library of Congress Cataloging-in-Publication Data
I see reality : twelve short stories about real life / edited by Grace Kendall. — First edition.
       pages cm
       Summary: "Popular young-adult authors weave together questions of identity, loss, and
    redemption into poignant tales for today's teens"—Provided by publisher.
       ISBN 978-0-374-30258-0 (hardback)
       ISBN 978-0-374-30259-7 (e-book)
       1. Teenagers—Fiction.   2. Short stories. [1. Short stories.   2. Interpersonal relations—
    Fiction.   3. High schools—Fiction.   4. Schools—Fiction.   5. Dating (Social customs)—
    Fiction.   6. Family life—Fiction.]   I. Kendall, Grace, editor.

PZ5.I24 2016
[Fic]—dc23

                                                              2015006007

Our books may be purchased for promotional, educational, or business use. Please contact your local
bookseller or the Macmillan Corporate and Premium Sales Department at (800) 221-7945 ext. 5442
or by e-mail at MacmillanSpecialMarkets@macmillan.com.

You can tell a book is real when your heart beats faster. Real books make you sweat. Cry, if no one is looking. Real books help you make sense of your crazy life. Real books tell it true, don't hold back, and make you stronger. But most of all, real books give you hope. Because it's not always going to be like this and books—the good ones, the real ones—show you how to make it better. Now.

—Laurie Halse Anderson, author of *Speak*

CONTENTS

I SEE
REALITY

THREE IMAGINARY CONVERSATIONS WITH YOU

Heather Demetrios

1

I'm breaking up with you today.

After two years, four months, three weeks, five days, and eight hours of being Gavin Davis's Girlfriend *I am breaking up with you*.

You won't see it coming. Your little high school girlfriend who never says no to you, the one who blows off her friends for your college keggers, the one who just sits there when you tell her she's a drag and that dating a girl in high school fucking sucks—*that* girl is Breaking Up With You.

I'm breaking up with you even though Christmas is next week and I already bought you a present it's too late to return.

I'm breaking up with you even though the thought of breaking up with you hurts.

This is how it will go down:

First we'll go to *The Nutcracker* because your mom bought us tickets as a Christmas present and I'll decide it'd be shitty not to go because she'll feel like I'm rejecting her and I only want to reject *you*. This will be a terrible decision, but I'll make it anyway because when we end, your parents—who see me as a daughter who's going to be in their family forever—will be collateral damage. I want them to hurt as little as possible. Obviously what I plan to do after the show is even more shitty, but at least your mom won't feel like she wasted the money. I just know that if I don't do this before Christmas, I never will. Because if I wait, you'll get me a sweet gift like you did last year (Who buys a first edition of a girl's favorite childhood book? *You.*)—and I won't be able to go through with it.

I *have* to do this.

I've pictured it a thousand times, a thousand different ways. This is one of them.

When you come to pick me up, I'll wonder if I should wait just a few more days because of how your eyes light up when you see me in my dress. I'll think about how in a few hours those eyes are going to be red-rimmed and pleading. (Note to self: wear something terrible.) And, of course, you'll be crazy hot, wearing a tie or something and the thought of you dressing up for another girl after we break up will make me insanely jealous, which is so stupid, but I won't be able to help it. Then I'll start psychoanalyzing what that means, like, if I feel jealous, then doesn't that prove that, deep down, I want to stay together? Meanwhile, I'll feel even more uncertain as I watch you play with my little brother, who you genuinely adore and constantly compare to the kid in *Jerry Maguire.* You'll call him little dude, which he loves. I'll see Sam kiss you on the cheek before we leave for the theater and you'll kiss him right back and it'll be the sweetest goddamn thing I've ever seen. Fuck you for that.

On the way to the theater, we'll get into a little argument and I'll feel vindicated. You're upset that my parents want me home by eleven. You'll sigh and shake your head, like you're the most put-upon boyfriend in the universe. "You're lucky I love you so much." Compliment and criticism rolled into one, as usual. But the thing is: I'll believe you. Because I know my parents are super strict and I'm a little bit of a prude. And because I still can't shake the awe that when we were in high school together, you chose me over girls who were so much prettier, so much *more*. I don't understand why you *still* choose me over college girls who are independent and flirty and fun. So, yeah, maybe I'm lucky. I'll still want to break up, though.

In the theater parking lot or going up the fancy staircase inside, I'll think about that day at the park, when we were on the swings and you said, *Jessa, you have no idea how hard it is to love you. But I can't stop. I won't stop.* You expanded on this. You went on and on about how hard I am to love with my negativity and my strict parents and my crazy ideas about chastity. You call me Eeyore, as in the depressive donkey from *Winnie-the-Pooh*, and not always affectionately. You say I'm a wet blanket and a tease and you don't care how much I get punished when I come home after curfew. You don't care what price I have to pay for us to be together. This is my ammunition and I have stored it carefully inside me: proof we are bad together.

After the show (you'll be a perfect gentleman, buying me the expensive souvenir program and kissing my neck), we'll be sitting in your mom's car outside McDonald's, our typical late-night-snack place. You'll have coffee, black. I'll have the McFlurry I don't want (You'll buy it for me even when I say not to because you hate eating or drinking or doing anything alone. You'll tell me I love McFlurries and that will be that).

"Hey, I know it's early, but . . ." You'll reach into your pocket and I'll shrink away. (*Crap! I thought I was doing this early enough!*) You'll hand me a long, thin velvet box. A jewelry box. I won't want to know what's inside, so I'll decide not to open it. This time, I won't let you trick me into staying together.

I'll shake my head. You'll think I'm being coy and you'll smile your sweet, sexy smile—not the cruel one—and you'll push it closer. (*Pushing*—you're so good at that, aren't you?) I'll hug the door of the car, keep my hands behind me. Your smile will slide off your face and, God, I won't be able to do this. Because I'll see your heart breaking, like you already know what's going to happen.

"What's up?" you'll ask. Your voice shakes a little, but you'll try to keep it casual.

For a minute, I won't be able to answer because you are so familiar to me and I'll start thinking (like I always do) about what it would be like not to have this: you, across from me, having our little traditions like coffee and McFlurries. I'll start wondering if this is the last time I'll ever sit in this car and my resolve will start to waver, just a little. I'll watch you for a minute because even then, preparing to break up with you, I can't stop looking. I can't stop wanting you.

Your hair is blond and the fluorescent parking lot lights make it gleam. I used to call you Prince Charming, before, when you were the popular senior captain of the water polo team, the guitar-playing god who noticed mousy little me and said *I'm taking you out tonight.* I'm only now realizing that wasn't a question. Technically, you never asked me out. You didn't give me the option of saying no.

At some point between leaving the theater and arriving at McDonald's you'll have grown tired of the tie and dress shirt and changed into the shirt I bought you two years ago, right after we got together. Just a stupid Hollister shirt, but you love it and sometimes ask me to sleep in it so it'll smell like me. It's faded now and has a hole near the shoulder and isn't that us, I'll want to say right then, *Isn't that us?*

I'll take a deep breath. "Wehavetobreakup."

You'll go still. Utterly, completely still.

You'll swallow. Look at the little box in your hand. A truck full of guys will rev past us and I'll jump. They'll swing into the drive-through and order half the menu while we sit there, staring at each other. You'll set my Christmas present on the dashboard.

"I'll kill myself if you break up with me."

You've never said this before, but when I imagine breaking up with you, I hear this. Because you said it to someone else, didn't you? And when she had the courage to do what I'm about to do . . . you *did* try to kill yourself. And, silly me, at the time I thought that was beautifully tragic. I saw you as the spurned lover, the ultimate romantic. God, what was I thinking? You were insane. I was reading too much Byron at the time, that must have been what it was.

I'll sit there in the passenger seat of your mom's sensible, slightly expensive car, the one with the seats that warm our asses, and my mind will freeze, like brain freeze only worse.

Kill.

Myself.

And then I'll get angry. Just imagining you doing this and putting your hypothetical suicide on me—it makes me so angry. Angry is good. I'll need to stay angry. That's how your ex did it and that's how I'll do it. I'll think about how you're saying this in a McDonald's parking lot. *In a McDonald's parking lot.* And I'll think: *Aren't you supposed to declare the intent to end your life in an abandoned alley or on a windswept moor—something just a little bit poetic?*

Then I'll be scared. Because . . . what if you mean it?

"No you won't." I'll whisper those words, as if saying them more quietly will calm the sharp-beaked thing inside you.

You'll take the keys out of the ignition and grip them in your palm and I am the keys, I am the one being held so tightly in your white-knuckled fist.

"Yes. I will." This will be said slowly, as if you were talking to a child, as if me still being in high school and you being in college automatically makes you the mature one. This is your Calm Boyfriend voice. I hate it now and I'll hate it then, too.

"I've thought about it before," you'll say. "I have a plan." You'll look at me. "You know I'll go through with it."

"Jesus, Gavin."

"Do you want to know how I'll do it?"

"No." Then I'll explode. "What the fuck is wrong with you? That's *sick.*"

"Do you think I like being like this?" You'll hit the steering wheel with your fist, hard. "It's your fault, for saying shit like that."

"I meant it. I don't want to be with you anymore." I'll start shaking and I won't be able to stop because I'll feel it slipping— me, my resolve, all of it.

"Then I mean it, too. Leave me, fine. I just hope you'll go to my funeral."

"What the *fuck*, Gavin?"

And I'll hear my best friend's voice, as though she's right in the car with us: *Stop letting him manipulate you, Jessa. He knows exactly what to say to keep you with him. He always does.*

It'll be quiet in the car for a long time and my mind will start to wander, to try to get away. In these almost-break-up moments it does that. I'll think about weird stuff like how I need to dust my bedroom or rework the thesis for a paper. But this night, I'll think of Adam. I know because I haven't been able to stop thinking about him for the past two weeks, since the cast party for the school play. You didn't want me to go. You wouldn't come because it was a "stupid high school party," but I finally put my foot down. It's my senior year and I want to enjoy it. I'm tired of ditching my friends because they're too lame for you.

So while you sit there imagining your suicide, I'll replay the cast party. It has become my happy place.

Adam is just my friend. I don't know if I like him as anything more than that, but when I was hanging out with him at the cast party, I realized that I might be feeling something for someone who isn't you. Nothing serious, just a tiny revelation that there are other guys in the world. I found myself wondering what it would be like to kiss him. Or even hold his hand. I didn't. I just imagined it.

Even though it was cold as hell, we sat by the edge of the pool at Jason Scheffer's house and talked all night and laughed so hard our stomachs hurt. For the first time in so long, I wasn't ashamed to be in high school. To be a kid. I told him about my necklaces, about how each one I make means something, has a story. I told him about how I collect the beads, sometimes for months or even years, and I wait until I can put the story of the necklace together. And the next day, he gave me a bead. Sea green with white swirls. He'd found it in the greenroom, when he was helping pack away costumes. It was such a small thing—literally, figuratively—but it felt huge. It was a gift from another guy and I kept it. *I kept it.* This scared the shit out of me, contemplating me with Adam or even just me without *us.* Our lives, after two years together, have become so entwined that the thought of unraveling you from me is almost as bad as the thought of never kissing someone else.

But back to the McDonald's parking lot. I need to picture all of this before you pick me up looking hot in your suit and kissing my little brother's cheek. I need to imagine the worst-case scenario because then when it happens, it'll be old news and you won't be able to shock me into staying together. So, you'll say you're going to kill yourself. I'll think about how I love you and how I don't want you to die. God, that's exactly what you'll want, isn't it? I love you+I don't want you to die=I don't break up with you. But they don't have to add up to that, they don't. I'll decide to be strong. I'll think about that bead and the possibility of dating lots of guys and not being Gavin Davis's Girlfriend, but instead . . . me. That will sound kinda nice. It will give me courage, that thought.

"Gavin." I'll put my hand over your fist. "I still love you. But I think we're over."

"You're my life," you'll say.

Wait. If you tell me this . . . what will I do? Because . . . I'm your life? Not your band or your friends at school or whatever, but . . . me? You've never told me that before. The doubt creeps in and I hate it because it's telling me to wait. *Just one more chance,* you always say. *I didn't know you felt that way . . . I can change . . . I'll give you more space . . .*

I'll stare at you. Your eyes will be more blue than green and I'll think that no one really knows that but me—how your eyes change color. Tonight they'll be sad and desperate and full of love.

"We can be so good together, you know that," you'll say. "Once you graduate, this will all be a bad dream, I promise."

Memories, so many. I'll think about the time you made me soup when I was sick and how you skipped the party for the water polo championships and stayed curled up next to me, risking the flu and reading me my favorite picture books. And of course I'll think about the first song you wrote me and how you serenaded me as I came out of math class. You even got some of the water polo team to back you up. (I still don't know how you convinced them to do that.) And, God, our first kiss: in the rain, against a wall in an alley—even now it makes me blush.

But I'll remember that there are words in my head, ones I've been practicing for months and never have the guts to say because right when I'm going to say them you do something wonderful. But I think I'll be able to say them tonight. *You can do this*, I'll tell myself.

"Gav. We aren't happy together." I want happy. So, so much.

"We fight. All the time. You're always in a bad mood when I'm around."

"Because your fucking parents never let me see you!"

"I'm seventeen!" I'll be yelling now. There's always a point where we start yelling and when you talk about my parents as *your fucking parents*, that will be the button you push that I can't ignore. I love my fucking parents. "I have a curfew. I have class every morning at seven thirty. I can't stay out until three a.m. like you do."

"Okay, I'm sorry. Jessa, please—"

You'll reach out and your fingers will touch the necklace around my neck. Because I'm feeling sentimental, I'll be wearing the one I made the week we got together, in a total frenzy, where each bead represented a daydream about you. Your fingers skim over the beads, over those fantasies about you and guilt, guilt, guilt because I'll think of that glass bead, which has been in my pocket since the day Adam gave it to me. How many times have I touched it over the past two weeks thinking, *what if, what if?*

"We have to break up," I'll say again. If I keep saying it, then maybe it will happen.

You'll turn away from me and take the necklace with you. I'll feel it go taut against my neck and then it'll be gone, beads everywhere, flying all over the car. I'll only know it's an accident by the shocked look on your face.

I'll have this thought: *I'll never be able to put it back together.* The necklace, us. Never, never.

You'll say you're sorry about a million times and we'll look at the beads and then, God, you'll be crying. Sobbing, almost. Fuck. Fuck. I'll want the anger to stay, but it's going . . . going . . .

"You're my soul mate, Jessa. We're supposed to be together. Forever. That was the deal."

Then you'll shatter right in front of me, just like you did when your dad said *I can't do this anymore* and walked out your front door with a suitcase in his hand. And I'll have to clean you up, put you back together. I'm glue. I'm glue.

"Don't be like him," you'll whisper. "Please, Jessa. I can't watch someone else walk away."

Ah, yes. The final nail in the coffin. This memory, this is what it always comes down to:

A fireplace. Christmas. Pretty lights and hot cocoa, you looking down at me.

"Don't ever leave me," you say.

"I won't."

Candy cane kisses, snow angels, mistletoe.

"Promise me." Your lips, so close to mine. "I don't want us to be like my parents. I want forever with you. Promise me, Jessa."

"I promise."

The memory will wash over me and your tears will cut me and I'll decide I won't do this to you, not after everything we've been through. I'll reach up and put my arms around you.

"I love you, I love you," I'll whisper. "I didn't mean it. I don't want to break up. I don't. I'm sorry."

You'll press your lips against mine and they'll be salty with tears and I'll breathe you in and even though my stomach will churn a little because a part of me has grown to hate the smell of your cologne, I'll let you pull me into your lap. We'll make out and we'll fall into it, so easy, so natural. And I'll tell myself I love you. I do. I do.

Your hands will cover my body like they own me. They stopped asking permission a long time ago. We'll go further than we ever have because I'll feel like I owe you, for putting you through this. I'll want to throw up. I'll want to kill myself.

"I'm glad I don't have to die tonight," you'll say a few hours later, as you drop me off at home, well past curfew. You'll smile, as though we're in on the same sick joke and, in a way, I guess we will be.

When I get inside, I'll put Adam's bead at the bottom of my jewelry box.

I won't look at it again.

2

I'm breaking up with you today.

I mean it this time.

I'm breaking up with you because when we took a "break" last month, you showed up on my doorstep every single night with a bouquet of flowers and a song you'd written about me, even though I told you I needed space.

I'm breaking up with you because instead of going to my senior prom tonight, I'm going to some stupid party your band is playing at.

I'm breaking up with you because I just found out that I got into your college and I'm scared that if I don't break up with you, I'll actually go there. And then you'll get me pregnant and I'll have to marry you and wear the scarves your sister knits me for the rest of my life and pretend to love you even though by then I'll hate you.

This is how it will go down:

I'll be standing against a wall at the party, by myself. Every time you come over, someone will pull you away and you'll give me an apologetic look and I'll turn into Stepford girlfriend and smile and say, "Go, go, I'm fine." I'll be dressed a little bit slutty because you like that, you like that it makes me look older. I'll wear too much makeup and the high heels will be killing my feet, but I'll wear them because you begged me to. You said they turn you on.

I'll check my cell and it'll be late, almost curfew. I won't want to check it too much because everyone will be posting pictures from prom and every time I see them I'll have to force myself not to cry. I'll think about what a mistake it was, coming to the party, and how I can never have another senior prom. The curfew thing will be stressing me out and I'll be so tired of pretending I'm actually going to drink the beer I'm holding in my hand.

By this point, I'll have told you I need to go five times already—five, I counted—but you'll keep saying, "Just a few more minutes." I'll feel jealous of the girls who hug you when they see you and are all starry-eyed over your sexy guitar playing and I'll wonder if I'm the biggest joke in the room. Finally you'll grab my hand and I'll think we might actually be leaving this time. "Guess we have to go," you'll say, all woe-is-me. "God, I can't wait until you graduate."

You are a broken record.

"You can come back," I'll say. "You know. After you drop me off."

A guy will come up as we're nearing the doors—the singer of the band that played before yours. Lead Singer smirks.

"Hey, Cradle Robber."

You'll have the good grace to bristle. But then I'll realize it's not for my benefit: it's for yours. I'll see how you're embarrassed for yourself, that you have to cart around a minor.

"Dude, shut the fuck up," you'll say.

"Just giving you a hard time, Gav." The guy will talk like I'm not there—they all do. Like I can't hear this conversation *about me*.

You'll smile and lean in closer to him and I won't be sure if I'm supposed to hear this—do you *want* me to hear this?

"The things she can do with her *mouth*." You'll shake your head, like you can't even begin to describe how good my blow jobs are and the lead singer guy raises his hand for a congratulatory fist bump and I will burn with shame, on fire, Joan of Arc burning, and you won't see it, you won't care and you'll do the fist bump and I'll hate you because I hate blow jobs and you know that, but you've never cared because, you say, "It's the least you can do." Like wanting to stay a virgin until I graduate is some kind of crime.

The guy will walk away and you'll turn to me and you must finally see the spontaneous combustion in front of you because you'll say, "Jessa. Don't be such a wet blanket. Jesus."

I'll practically run out of there, which is pretty hard to do in my too-high heels. You'll catch me halfway down the street and

I'll be crying by then and you'll hold me to you and you won't let go.

"I'm sorry," you'll whisper. "I'm such a dick. I'm sorry. He just got under my skin and I'm pissed I have to take you home. I miss you."

I'll smell the beer on your breath and the cigarettes on your T-shirt and it'll give me enough strength to push you away from me.

"No. I'm done."

I'll whip out my phone and dial my best friend. I'm calling her to pick me up—she said she'd ditch her prom date if I needed her to.

"Don't," you'll say, reaching for the phone. "Let me take you home."

"No." My voice will be a growl and it'll feel so good to say the one word that's been absent from my vocabulary for so long. I'll hold on to the phone like it's a can of pepper spray.

"*Jessa.*" Your voice will break and there's fear in it, real fear, and I'll suddenly get why you won't let me do this, no matter how hard I try.

"The only reason you're staying with me," I'll say, savoring each word, "is because you don't want to be alone. You're *afraid* to be alone."

"That's not true."

But I can finally admit it to myself. I hope it goes down like this tonight because I want to say these words to you so bad. They're crawling up my throat. I want to vomit them all over you. I want you to smell like them for days afterward.

"We're not soul mates," I'll say. "I'm your rebound. You and Genna broke up and then there I was, conveniently worshipping at your feet, and so you—"

"That's bullshit." You'll move closer to me, but I'll back away. Maybe I'm going too far with this fantasy, but it's like a scene in a movie and I want to be the badass heroine who tells the jerk boyfriend to fuck off. "I was into you way before Genna and I broke up. I know you're mad, but stop being such a bitch."

This won't hurt as much as it should because you've said it before, in various ways: *fucking bitch, goddamn bitch.* Say it enough and it doesn't hurt anymore. That's what I tell myself, anyway.

"You didn't even know my *name* before you guys broke up—"

It'll look like I've got you there, but you're smart, so smart.

You'll say: "What about the shooting star?"

That goddamn star. It's why I've stayed with you so long.

We're lying on the ratty old picnic blanket your parents keep in the backyard. I'm feeling so unbelievably lucky that Gavin Davis wants to make out with me under the stars. Your parents aren't home, but I'm terrified they'll come and catch this girl they've never met wearing nothing but a bra and way too short skirt that their son is currently putting his hands under.

"Maybe . . . um . . . we shouldn't . . ." I try to get the words out but stars, and fingers, and your lips, your lips.

Your mouth is against my ear and you whisper, "We definitely should."

I pull away from you, confused. Thinking how dumb I am, that maybe you just want to hook up. I'm not that girl. I can't be—even for you.

"Gavin. I really like you."

"I don't like you." Everything turns to ice, but then you smile and

*reach for me and your eyes get glassy and your voice is so soft when
you say, "I love you."*

*I don't realize that you're too good at one-liners and romantic
moments. I think it's just for me. That I somehow inspire it all.*

*Later, we lie on our backs, staring at the sky. And then—a shoot-
ing star. We gasp at the same time and you reach out and grip my
hand.*

"I've never seen one before," I say.

You smile. "It's a sign."

"Of what?"

"That we're meant to be together."

"It wasn't a sign," I'll say. I'm tired of you using the star to build
a case for our cosmic love. I'm over it. "A shooting star is just a
rock."

Your eyes will narrow in that look that tells me you're going to
say something especially cruel. "Those girls in there—" You point
back toward the party. "Do you know how many of them have
tried to hook up with me since I started going to school here?
They don't have curfews. They're on birth control. They don't
give a damn what Mommy and Daddy think and they have their
own fucking apartments."

"Great, then as soon as we break up, you can go fuck all of
them in their fucking apartments!"

Your eyes will widen—you can't believe I've got it in me to say
any of that, can you? But then your lips will turn up and . . .
and . . . I'll see that you're . . . amused—*what?* What. The. Fuck.
I'll be so mad I could spit, but you'll start cracking up and suddenly I'll feel ridiculous.

"Stop laughing at me," I'll say. I'll still be clutching my phone and I'll need to call Erin, I'll need to call her and tell her to pick me up.

"I'm not laughing at you!"

I'll look and it's true—you'll be smiling like the Gavin I fell for, back when we were both in high school. You'll lay your palms against my cheeks and it'll be like a scene from a movie where people get together in the end.

"I'm so in love with you, Jessa, you have no idea."

"What?"

Bingo. You got me.

Because I'll be so confused. Two seconds ago you were listing all the reasons dating me is a total buzzkill. Then you swoop in with a romantic declaration.

You'll lean closer and I'll hate that my body responds to that. How can I still want you?

"I'm sorry."

You'll whisper the words. Bedroom talk. "I said that thing about the girls to see if you'd be jealous. I had to know if you still . . . if you still wanted me."

Your mind games. God, you're so good at keeping me off balance.

"That's *messed up*, Gavin!" I'll actually hit you with my purse and it'll feel good to hear the smack of the leather against your skin.

But you'll smile. "You're so goddamn sexy when you're mad. You're like this fierce goddess—"

"Gavin, stop. Just stop, okay?"

I'll step away from you. Erin told me I had to do it tonight.

That this was the final straw. The one that broke the camel's back. The . . . the . . . oh God, whatever all those expressions are, this is all of that.

"No more. No more this or us or . . . just. No more. Please." I'll be begging you. Please let me end this. Please, please.

You'll suddenly turn serious. "I'm sorry about the prom. I know you wanted to go. I just . . . Jessa, I'm twenty years old. Like, I love you and I want to make you happy, but I can't go to a high school prom."

"And that's fine, I get it, but this was *my* prom and I'll never have another one—"

"I don't think it's crazy for me to be uncomfortable with the idea of you dancing with other guys all night."

I'll throw up my hands, frustrated. "Gavin, I told you I was going to dance with my friends as a group and sit out all the slow songs."

"I was gonna tell you to go without me," you'll say. "I really was. I knew how much it meant to you and I thought, *There's nothing to worry about—you trust her.* But then I saw those pictures."

I know you'll bring this up because it's been our daily argument for the past two weeks.

You saw the pictures from the cast party on my phone and how Adam and I were always sitting next to each other, laughing. Even though it was five months ago and *nothing fucking happened*, you completely freaked out. Wouldn't give me my phone back until you searched through my emails. And I let you. *I let you.* Because I don't know how to say no to you.

"That's bullshit," I'll say, totally pissed off. "Like I've told you a million times, I have never done anything wrong—I would never cheat on you." This is the truth.

"I saw the way you were looking at each other in those pictures."

"You saw pictures of me sitting next to a guy who wasn't you and decided there was something going on—*which there isn't*," I'll say. "We go to school together every day. If I wanted to cheat on you, I could have. So what does it matter if I go to prom and he's there?"

"You'll dance with him, for one."

"His name is Adam, not *him*, and no, I wouldn't have, because he has his own prom date—"

"So the only reason you wouldn't dance with him is because he has a date."

"That's not what I meant," I'll say. "You're putting words in my mouth."

I'll take off my heels because my feet will be in excruciating pain and I'll throw the shoes against the brick wall we're standing next to but will wish I could throw them at you because here we are, spinning on a merry-go-round from hell.

"Stop being such a child," you'll snap.

"If I'm such a child, then why are you with me?" I'll feel hopeful when I say this—maybe you'll be pissed off enough to break up with me. Maybe I won't have to do it.

You'll shake your head. "Look, I don't want to argue anymore. I'm just saying, shit happens on prom night and that's why I wanted to keep you close, all right?" You'll look down at me, slightly paternal. "I'm not okay with the possibility of my girlfriend screwing some guy from her drama class on prom night because she had too much to drink and he looked good in his tux."

"I don't even drink!" I'll yell. Then I'll lower my voice because we're in public and there are some things you don't shout from the rooftops, such as: "And I'm a virgin. And I'm well aware of the fact that I have a boyfriend and that means something to me, like not screwing other guys on prom night."

I'll start to walk away. Screw the heels, I'll be barefoot, heading toward the bus stop. But you'll run after me, suddenly panicked.

"Jessa." You'll grab my arm and I'll try to shake you off, but you're holding on too tight. I'll probably have a bruise. "Okay, I'm sorry." Your voice will go soft. "Is that what you want to hear? I'm sorry I didn't trust you, I'm sorry I love you so much. I'm sorry."

"Gavin . . ."

"Listen. I know I have to work on the jealousy thing. It just makes me crazy, not being able to be with you—your parents, your schedule." I'll try to pull away, but I'm starting to lose steam. "If you're not happy by the end of the summer, then okay, you can leave me. But you owe us the summer at least."

When I told you that after I graduate, I won't have a curfew anymore, you literally jumped in the air and shouted, a huge smile spreading across your face. I'll remember that moment and the doubt will creep in.

"It's just been so hard lately," I'll whisper. Suddenly I'll feel so tired. I won't have the energy to have this same fight again.

"I know. But I'm telling you, it's going to be so great. *We're* going to be so great."

Those one-liners of yours get me every time, make me feel like I'm on-screen, people watching us as they eat popcorn. But this isn't a movie, it's my life and it sucks.

"I don't know, Gav. It just feels like . . . we can't fix this."

There's a moment of silence, and I'll think I'm finally getting through to you, but then you'll say: "Do you want to know what I did last weekend, when you were studying for finals?" You'll tilt my chin up, so that you can look in my eyes. "I went ring shopping."

I'll go hot, then cold. "What?"

"I didn't buy it yet," you'll say. "Need to save more money. But I have it all planned out, how I'll ask you." You'll be bashful then, a soft, secret smile playing on your face. The ice around my heart will start melting. Not in a good way, in a global-warming way. But it's not frozen anymore and that's all that matters in this moment. "Jessa, I want to spend the rest of my life with you."

All that frustration in my chest will explode, silently, so only I'll know it's happening. Everything will feel dark and bad and hopeless inside me and I'll sit right there on the sidewalk and bury my head in my hands. I won't know if I'm crying because right at that moment my friends are at prom, having the night of their lives, or because I'll know that we're not breaking up. Not then, maybe not ever.

You'll reach down and pick me up and cradle me against you (*cradle robber*), thinking I'm crying from happiness.

I'll be dead weight.

3

I'm breaking up with you today.

I'm wearing a necklace made of beads, each one a promise to myself that I will break up with you. The first bead is the one Adam gave me, way back when, the sea-green one with the white swirls.

I'm breaking up with you even though you might try to kill yourself (and I don't think you will—you love yourself too much to do that).

I'm breaking up with you right before graduation. Because I won't let you ruin this day. I won't let you take one more thing away from me.

I'm breaking up with you because I'm going to spend the whole summer with the friends I've neglected for the past two years. And then I'll go to a college far away. I'll be by myself for a while. Then I'll find someone I don't want to break up with.

This is how it will go down:

You'll get my text and a few minutes later, you'll be walking toward me.

I'll have asked you to meet me in the high school parking lot because it's a public place. Because I don't trust you anymore. I'm scared to be alone with you. My best friend will be standing a few feet away. She has promised to break up with you for me, if I don't do it. I gave her permission to drag me away from you, if need be. She would do it, too.

You'll smile when you see me and dance a little jig because this is the day we've been waiting for. But I'm going to make it the worst day of your life. I'll be sick with nerves and sad and I'll hate that a part of me still loves you, still lifts a little when you walk toward me with that slacker shuffle.

"How's my girl?" you'll say when you reach me.

I'll feel the cracks spreading through my heart as it starts to break. You'll be wearing the tie I bought you—the one with the skull and crossbones. I know you love it. I know you're wearing it for me. "Jessa?"

I'll grip the necklace. It's too late for Adam and me, but I'm okay with that. Because it's not too late for *me*. It feels good to be selfish, but it's hard.

I'll open my mouth, but the words won't come. Despite everything, I won't want to break your heart. And I won't want you to break mine. I just want us to . . . drift away from each other. I'll wish there didn't have to be words. Or that you, for once, could be the one who has to say the hard thing.

"What happened?" you'll ask. You are Concerned Boyfriend. I am Asshole Girlfriend.

Tears will be filling my eyes by this point and I'll shake my head. I'll think about how Erin will have to put more bobby pins in my hair because my mortarboard will be slipping off.

Your hands will grip my arms, your skin warm on mine. "Baby, what's wrong?"

Oh, God, you'll think it's not you, that there was some kind of graduation drama. Your voice will be sweet and I'll know you want to protect me and it'll be too much. The end of high school, the end of us. The beginning of everything else. *I don't know if I can do this.* I'll turn my head and see Erin hiding behind someone's SUV. It'll make me feel strong, knowing someone has my back.

"We're breaking up. Right now. Please don't say anything." The words will come out in a rush and sweat will be dripping off me and *Please, God, please let me really do it this time.*

You have no idea how hard it is to love you.

You're such a wet blanket.

Tease.

Bitch.

Stop being such a child.

You're lucky I love you so much.

You'll stare at me. For once, you won't say a word. Because you'll know I mean it this time.

And then I'll walk away from you.

I won't look back.

THE DOWNSIDE OF FABULOUS

Kristin Elizabeth Clark

The classification of living things is called taxonomy," Mr. Megars says, writing the word on the whiteboard at the front of the classroom. He's left-handed, so *taxonomy* gets smeary and blurred by the time he gets to the *y*.

I'm pretty sure generations of tenth graders have been fooled into thinking their eyesight is going as a result of sitting in this guy's class.

"This system was developed in the 1700s by Carl Linnaeus in order to identify and classify every living thing," he explains. "Because labels are important."

I add two Xs for eyes on the sketch I'm making of a bored kid sitting at a lab table. It's got a manga feel to it that I'm a little stoked by.

My stomach rumbles, and next to me Liz mimics the noise barely audibly. Is it my fault bio is just before lunch? I'm a big guy, I get hungry! Mentally, I'm already piling into Gordon Alexander's Suburban with the other theater tech crew geeks and Liz, if she's not off eating with other people. She's one of those rare individuals who navigate the minefield of high school cliques without getting her legs blown off.

"Here, Chris," she whispers, sliding me a bite-sized Mars bar under the table.

Megars glances back toward us. I palm the candy and sit up straight. My mom's a teacher and her biggest complaint is students who sit in her class looking bored. I suspect her of grading those students harder. I try to at least give the appearance of looking alert because I'm screwed if I don't bring home straight As.

He turns back to write something else.

Megars is dull, but his class does have a couple of saving graces. The first is that he doesn't use a seating chart, which means I can sit next to Liz: provider of Mars bars when I'm hungry, next-door neighbor since kindergarten, best friend, and confidant. Up until recently, there was absolutely nothing one of us didn't know about the other.

"Using man as an example, here's how it goes," Megars says, drawing a fuzzy pyramid. At the bottom he writes *Kingdom, Animalia*. On the next line up he writes *Phylum, Chordata*.

I look down at the handout, which has the same pyramid and says the same thing. I sketch the River Nile in the margin, add a boat, and then make the bored-looking kid the captain.

Megars continues up the pyramid through class, order, and family. When he gets to genus, the word is *homo*. Two tables over, Joe Trimble snickers. I look up just in time to see Tom Waters (saving grace number two) turn around and raise an eyebrow at Joe. The message is clear.

Not chill.

Joe looks down at his table and the tips of his ears redden.

That is one powerful eyebrow, I think.

There's just something about Tom—a worldly air to every-thing he does. His mom's a travel writer and his dad's a photog-rapher and they're always taking Tom out of school to go with them to places like India and Japan. Sometimes for months at a time.

In fact, that happened so often in elementary and middle school, he's actually a year older than anyone else in our class. But when being held back is the result of hiking in Cameroon from February to May . . . Well, let's just say that Tom's managed to even make repeating eighth grade seem like the sophisticated thing to do.

He's on the student council, he's the lead in every drama club musical (right now it's *Guys and Dolls*), and he made var-sity tennis his freshman year. He also started the Diversity Task Force, devoted to spreading the gospel of inclusiveness to our school.

The club is popular because Tom is popular.

He's also gay.

"You'll be working with your partner on making posters of three different phylogenetic trees and labeling them with the Lin-naean classification system," Megars says.

I continue to study Mr. Saving Grace Number Two. He's got on a vintage white tux jacket. He wears it a lot, probably because it fits perfectly across his broad shoulders. Sandy blond curls just touch the collar, and from this angle I can see the slight scruff of facial hair along his square jaw. I think about its texture, about touching it, and how it would feel under my fingers . . . I shut my eyes for a second.

"The only requirement is that one of the trees must be that of humans. As for the others, whatever floats your boat."

What floats my boat is Tom Waters.

At first I thought my attraction to other guys might be just a phase. You know, something some guys go through on their way to getting hot for girls. Last summer though, Liz and I took her mom's Volvo to the basketball team car wash. Cheerleaders were out helping them, and Liz made some snarky observation about the bikini Daria Evans was wearing.

I didn't see the bikini. I was too busy noticing the little river of water running down the sharply defined bicep crease on point guard Rob Kendal's Michelangelo-worthy arm.

That's when I realized that three years is a ridunkulous amount of time for a phase to last.

I'm not one for big announcements, so even when I realized I was definitely gay, I just figured I'd wait until there was a reason to come out. In fact, it's now been four months and I've told no one, even though I know my parents will be fine with it.

When I was eleven or so, my Aunt Jen made the mistake of telling me I was going to grow up to make some woman very happy. My mom jumped all over her, saying that I was going to make some *person* happy, and that she wasn't going to stand for her kid's indoctrination into heteronormativity. (A word I only recently looked up.)

"Neatness counts, as does obvious effort." Megars could not sound more bored. "In the next couple of days, choose your partner and get with them to plan. Today is Monday, posters are due a week from Thursday; that gives you plenty of time. I'll be able to tell if you waited until the last minute."

Tom leans sideways to grab a book from his backpack on the floor, exposing a few inches of tanned wrist. I stare for a second, then snap my head toward Liz because I have this absurd notion that she, the person I'm closest to in the world, would have caught that one-second stare and realized what it meant.

Liz just looks at me like *what?*

Clearly telepathy is not one of my superpowers. I look back over at Tom, who may or may not know I'm even alive. I manage to keep a sigh from escaping my lips.

Of course Liz'll be the first person I'll come out to.

I think I finally have a reason to do it.

I don't believe you."

Liz and I are sitting on beanbag chairs in her den, controllers in our hands, Converse shoes in a heap next to us. (Mine are a little bigger and a lot rattier than hers. She also claims mine smell, but it's nothing I've ever noticed.) She unpauses the game (Mordock's Giant) and goes back to blowing up gnomes, like it's the end of the conversation.

I can only stare at her.

Of all the possible responses I'd imagined, this is one I never considered.

I'd prepared myself for "It's probably a phase." You know, because I actually thought that myself for the aforementioned three years. (Call me slow.) I'd prepared myself for "When did you decide you were gay?" To which I had my response ready: "When did you decide you were straight?" I even prepared myself for a squirmy made-for-TV-movie moment of a hug and a promise of support. But "I don't believe you"?

I don't know what to do with that except pause the game again, before any fireballs can come out of the trees and decimate me.

"What? It's true!"

"Pretending to be gay isn't funny." Liz's dark eyebrows are raised and wisps of hair are falling across her furrowed forehead. Her exasperation is as plain as the piercing in her nose.

"I'm not pretending!"

"You can't be gay." Again, like *end of discussion.*

She starts to unpause the game. I turn it off.

"Why would you say that?"

"Well." She exhales dramatically and looks up at the ceiling like someone spray-painted a cheat sheet up there. "There was that time in seventh grade, when we . . ." She lets the sentence trail off.

An embarrassing memory zaps my neurons. It was at Sam Nesbaugh's end-of-the-year party. I spent the day in the pool wrestling with the other guys and the occasional girl who'd gotten thrown in. When it got dark, the kids who were still there played spin the bottle. The fact that Liz and I kissed was eclipsed by the memory of how I'd spent the day in the water with a half husker, hoping no one else noticed.

The smug look on Liz's face says she thinks she's stumped me somehow. Then I remember what she's talking about.

"For crying out loud! That was spin the bottle! What was I

going to do? Refuse to play? And we both thought it was gross!" I remind her.

We'd walked home together and agreed that kissing each other was a never-to-be-repeated experiment.

Wait. Am I the only one who thought it was gross?

Liz must read my mind (this time) because she punches me. Hard.

"Don't even think it," she says. "I most certainly have not been sitting around for three years pining over you and that kiss. I just don't think you're gay."

"I'm a guy. I like guys. How is that not gay?"

Liz brushes over this fact like it's a glitch in the screen. "You play video games. Sometimes obsessively."

"So do you!" Am I really arguing this with her?

"True. But in me it's unexpected, maybe even charming," she says.

"Don't make me puke. Plus, there *are* Gay-mers."

"You're always on the tech crew, never the stage."

"Now you're just being stupid! Besides, there *are* gay techies; Emily Lupine stage-manages every show."

"One. One gay techie. And she's a girl," Liz says. "Also, you slouch." Then she points to the stains on the front of my plain white T-shirt. "And sorry, but you're a slob."

I look down at my dirty shirt. My stomach pooches a little over my jeans.

"This proves nothing except that my hot sauce packet exploded at lunch!"

"Pffftttt—and you didn't rush home to change immediately."

What am I doing here, trying to assert my . . . gaytivity? And who the hell does Liz think she is to question me? I wrap the cord around my controller and slam it down on the TV stand.

"I wanted you to know this thing." I raise my voice. "This one really important thing about me. I didn't realize I'd have to pass the gay SAT to get your tiny mind to accept it!"

Liz stands up and drops her controller to the ground. "I am *not* small-minded!" she snaps, and then, "Your mom's calling you." This is our code for "time for you to leave." It's usually only invoked in jest, but Liz's face is flushed and I know she means it.

Which is more than fine by me.

I shove my binder into my backpack. We haven't even discussed the bio assignment.

"Clearly leaving," I say, grabbing my shoes and opening the sliding glass door that leads to her backyard. Barefoot, I get to the side gate that leads to mine.

"Thanks for the support," I yell.

The next morning I leave for school early in order to avoid walking with Liz. In bio, when I see she's claimed our usual table, I pass by her without a word. I'm suddenly conscious of the fact that my show shirt from last year (the front says *tech crew*, the back says *techies do it in the dark*) is a little tight, and I have to do that annoying tug-to-make-sure-it-stays-down-over-the-gut thing. I'm also suddenly conscious of the way I'm carrying myself. Liz accused me of being a sloucher, and it's true, I slouch.

But that doesn't make me straight.

I grab an open table near the front of the room, sit down, and keep my eyes straight ahead like I'm fascinated by the smeary whiteboard notes left over from Megars's last class. I will not look back. I will not look back.

Someone slides onto the stool next to me and leans his arm on the table. I don't need to turn my head to know who it is. No one else I know has that exact shade of blond down on his forearm, and even if he did, no one else's blond forearm down could cause the reaction in my gut that *this* blond forearm down is causing.

"Okay if I sit here?" Tom asks.

"Positutely!" The second that word's out of my mouth, I would give anything for a time machine. I would go back to the day of my birth and rip out my tongue in order to keep it from ever uttering something so asinine.

Tom doesn't seem to notice though. He's checking out my binder, the one with the sketch of the kid with x-ed out eyes on it.

"Hey, did you draw this?" he asks.

"Um yeah, it's not . . ." He doesn't wait for me to tell him it's not my best work, it's just a doodle.

"This is great!" he says. "You really captured something there." He glances behind us. Before I can stop myself, I look back to see what he's looking at.

Liz sees me and makes her *what?* face.

We both turn back around.

"Fight with the girlfriend?" Tom asks.

"She's not, uh, we're not . . ." I'm tongue-tied. I finally come up with, "Nah, I just needed to move closer to the board."

I point to Megars's blurry handwork. "I think I'm going blind. That look fuzzy to you?"

Tom laughs. "I thought my contacts were dirty."

The bell rings. Megars takes roll and announces we'll be watching something called *The Private Life of Plants*. He pulls down the screen and turns off the lights.

"Oh my God," Tom whispers. "It's happened! I can't see!"

I laugh. And like him even more. Worldly, sophisticated, *and* a doofy sense of humor. An unlikely combo I'd never imagined until Tom.

For the next fifty minutes, I'm conscious of the heat of his arm, inches from mine on the table. Every once in a while one of us will make a stupid joke about the film. If possible, his jokes are even stupider than mine.

The bell rings just as the movie ends. Someone turns on the lights, and people start grabbing their stuff and shuffling out. Tom blinks, clearly coming out from the semistupor that educational films are designed to put their (helplessly captive) audience in.

I'm wide-awake.

"Hey," he says, slowly hefting his backpack over one perfectly formed shoulder. "Want to do the classification poster together? I can't draw, but I'm good at lettering and at looking things up."

Mute, I nod, and then shrug both my less-than-perfectly-formed shoulders, like *no big deal*.

"I have tennis right after school and rehearsal at seven o'clock, but if you come over at four thirty, we can do it in between," he says. He pulls out his phone and takes my digits so he can text me his address.

I leave bio feeling high.

Until Liz catches up with me on my way out of the building.

"Hey," she says.

"Hey," I say in a monotone that would make Megars proud.

She touches my arm. "Look, I'm sorry."

"Mmmhhmmm," I say, heading for the parking lot. Other people jostle around us in the mad rush to get to their cars. Lunch is only thirty-five minutes long.

Liz grabs me. "Really, I was just surprised!" She doesn't bother to lower her voice. "It never in a million years would have occurred to me that you're gay."

"Oh, I totally knew Chris was gay," Gordon says from behind us. We both whip around, Liz's hand on her mouth about five seconds too late.

My instamortification that he overheard is weirdly enough replaced by (brief but insane) instagratitude that he recognizes I'm gay.

"Really?" I ask.

"Oh, totally!" He laughs.

"How?" Liz demands.

Gordon's mouth shuts. His eyes do that shifty anime-ninja thing.

A car peels out of the lot.

"Um, you're serious?" he asks. "I thought you were joking."

The words "Yes, I'm serious" grind out through my clenched molars.

"Huh." Gordon looks down at his keys like he's never seen them before. He jangles them a little in his hand. "You just don't . . ."

"What?" I demand, even though I think I know what.

"It's cool." He scratches the back of his neck, then tilts his head. "But you just don't *seem* gay."

"Exactly!" Liz says.

Without a word I turn around and head back toward school. Freshmen aren't allowed off campus at lunch. I'll eat crap food out of the vending machine behind the theater with them today.

A t four fifteen I leave a note telling my mom where I'm going, then head over to Tom's. He lives a good six blocks from me and it's Indian summer. Between the heat, my angry imaginary conversation with Liz, and my flirty imaginary conversation with Tom, I'm pretty sweaty by the time I get there.

I walk through a courtyard to get to the huge front door. I'm doing a surreptitious little sniff of my pits before ringing the bell when the door swings open and Tom is standing there. Caught, I pretend to be looking down (sideways) at a cast-iron doorstop in the shape of a poodle.

"Cool house," I say, stepping into the front room, which is cavernous. To my right, an indoor fountain trickles. One entire wall is covered in books, and a huge statue of Buddha dominates the space.

"Thanks." Tom leads me through an arched doorway toward the back of the house. "We can snag supplies from my dad's studio, he won't care."

"He's not home?"

"Nah, he and my mom went out mushroom foraging. They won't be back until tonight."

"Mushroom foraging? Is that a thing?" I ask.

"It is for my parents," Tom says, shaking his head. "I don't get it."

"Me neither," I say. And then take a chance. "But your dad sounds like a fungi!"

Tom bursts out laughing. "That was the worst joke ever!"

"And yet, you laughed," I say, shaking my finger at him in what I hope is a playful, maybe even flirtatious way.

We continue on through the kitchen (also huge) and out the back door to a little house behind the big one. Inside, prints and notes cover every available surface. Studio lights and tripods lean together in one corner. There's a corkboard covered in newspaper clippings I'm too far away to read, and several crowded book-shelves line the back wall.

Tom opens the door to a closet and starts pawing through paper supplies while I check out some mounted photographs leaning against a wall. They're of landmarks I recognize, despite never having been to any of them. There's the Eiffel Tower, the Christ of the Andes, the Colosseum. I come across a picture of Tom himself, standing on a huge stone walkway. Jagged green hills loom in the background.

"Is this the Great Wall of China?"

Tom pulls out a poster-sized piece of thick white paper. He glances over at me and shrugs. "It's the Pretty Okay Wall of China."

I guess the very definition of worldly is someone who can be blasé about the Great Wall of China. I shake my head.

"Hey, I laughed at your worst joke, the least you could do is laugh at my best," he complains in a mock-whiny voice.

It makes me smile, but I can't think of a clever comeback, so instead I ask, "Don't you like traveling?"

"Some of it's okay." He closes the closet door. "But would you want to spend months at a time with just your parents and their friends?"

We go back into the main house and set up at the kitchen table. We decide to use the grizzly bear and the tulip for our phylogenetic tree, and Tom sits next to me. He opens a laptop so we can look up their classification and Latin names.

"Also, I've always wanted a dog," he says, and it takes me a second to realize we're continuing the conversation about travel. "But my parents say we're never home enough."

"A dog, huh." I start to sketch. Tom's so close I can smell him.

In a good way.

"You could get a poodle," I say, thinking of the iron doorstop. "One of those little tiny ones that fits inside its own little purse so you could take it with you."

There's silence, and when I look up from my drawing Tom has a weird look on his face.

He gets up and goes to the refrigerator. He grabs a little bottle of Perrier but doesn't offer me one.

"I was thinking more like a Rottweiler," he says, pulling the laptop to the other end of the table and sitting down in front of it.

We don't talk much after that, except about where to put different categories on the tree. When it's time for Tom to get ready for rehearsal, we're only two-thirds of the way through.

I get home to a note from my parents, reminding me that it's their date night and that they won't be back until later.

I grab a Coke, fill a bowl with Cheez-Its for dinner, and head upstairs, my mind on Tom. I think I'm alone in the house, so when I open my bedroom door, I'm incredibly startled to see Liz. I yelp, and the crackers go flying.

She jumps up. "Sorry! Sorry! Sorry! I didn't mean to scare you!"

Jesus! She should get a job as a hospital defibrillator; my heart is beating like crazy. "What are you doing here?"

"I grabbed the key from the flowerpot as soon as your parents left." Her voice is a little choky and her nostrils are red. "I wanted to let you know how bad I feel about everything."

She points to a banner I didn't notice in the midst of my heart failure. It's stretched across the window and spells out *I'm SO Sorry* in foot-high letters.

I don't say anything. Instead I put the Coke on my dresser and start picking up the crackers that went skittering across the hardwood floor.

She kneels down to help. "I know I should have just shut up and listened when you came out to me, instead of criticizing you." She pauses, one hand on the bowl, her eyes welling up. "I'm a shitty friend."

God, I hate it when she cries. I scoop the last of the Cheez-Its into the bowl, walk over to my desk, and grab her a Kleenex.

She takes it and dabs under her eyes, smearing her mascara.

I put the bowl on my dresser next to the Coke. Liz sits back down at my desk, and I'm about to sit on my bed, when she clears her throat and says, "But in my defense, Gordon didn't believe it either."

This is too much! "Gordon, who shouldn't've known until *I* told him!" I explode.

She tears up again. "I know! I'm the worst friend ever."

Ordinarily I'd hug her, but I'm not there yet. I do hand her another tissue and stand there awkwardly while she cries. I know that's not helpful, but it's what I can manage at the moment.

After a minute she blows her nose, and finally I sit.

She stares down at the Kleenex. "I have a plan to make it up to you," she says quietly.

"Does this involve inducing amnesia in Gordon so I can tell him myself?"

She crumples a little next to me. "I wish I could, but since I can't . . . you like Tom Waters, don't you?"

I give her a sideways look. I will admit nothing.

She starts shredding one of the tissues. Not the snot-rag one.

"You don't have to admit it, but I watched you in bio together today."

I grunt. It's not a commitment.

"So here's the thing. You don't seem gay. But if you are," she says, and before I can react to the *if* she corrects herself. "*Since* you are, you're eventually going to want to do something about it. If you want to make sure Tom knows you're gay, you need to be more obvious about it, you know? Make your sexual orientation more apparent."

"Really," I say, in that tone that means this isn't a question.

She looks at me, almost pityingly. "Chris, I've heard of gaydar, and I don't want to hurt your feelings, but I'm pretty sure you don't set that off in anyone."

She gets up from my desk and sits next to me on the bed. "If we give you a makeover, it'll be more obvious." She punches me in the arm.

I guess this violence is meant to prove that she's back to her usual self.

"And I have the most brilliant idea!" she says, bouncing a little. "We'll unveil the Fabulous New You at Lillian's party on Friday!"

Lillian Bruner, president of the drama club, has a get-together once a semester. In theory it's a meeting to talk about drama club business, but really it's a parent-sanctioned excuse to have people over. It's one of the few times the techies and the actors really mingle. Tom is sure to be there.

"Once we've made you over, he'll be dazzled, and the rest will be history."

"That is the dumbest idea I've ever heard," I tell her.

And I mean it.

The next day, though, I walk into bio to see that Tom has claimed a seat next to Alex Lee. Alex may or may not be gay, but he wears collared shirts and penny loafers, and he has a killer smile.

I sit down next to Liz at our old lab table.

"Okay." I give in. "Transform me to fabulous."

By late Thursday afternoon, I have had just about enough. We're headed toward our third vintage clothing store of the day. After what feels like a gazillion hours spent shopping, I am now the owner of three button-down shirts and a pair of skinny (well, skinny for me) jeans. For the last two hours Liz has jabbered my ears off about *Real Housewives* and designer sunglasses. These topics have never before interested either of us, but Liz thinks I should know about them now in order to better convey my gayness.

"Did you listen to the playlist I made you?" she asks.

"Yeah," I tell her, even though I only listened to half of it. It's not that I'm not into music, but I just can't seem to get into Lady Gaga or the soundtrack to *Moulin Rouge!*

"Good. Tonight I'll send you the list of witty things you can say tomorrow to show off your snarky sense of humor."

"*Your* snarky sense of humor," I grumble.

But Tom sat next to Alex in bio again today, and he blew me off when I asked if we could finish the poster this weekend. I'm committed to Liz's plan.

A bell on the door tinkles when we walk into The Happy Dragon Consignment Store. A musty odor is the first thing I notice.

"Vintage stores cost more than Goodwill, but don't smell that much better," I complain. "And the Goodwill smells like poverty."

Liz laughs and says, "Now you're getting the hang of it."

This store has rows of clothing on old-fashioned wooden bars, and mirrors at the end of the aisles that are pitted and speckled with age. There's a bored-looking clerk behind the counter, and a stuffed owl sitting on what looks like an old dresser. I step closer to take a look (at the owl, not the clerk) but Liz grabs my arm.

"*That is perfect!*" she squeals, pointing toward the back of the store. She drags me toward a white tuxedo jacket that's hanging face-out on the wall next to the dressing room. It's an exact replica of the one Tom wears, except that it's several sizes bigger than his.

Liz grabs it off the hook and hands it to me.

"Try it on," she orders.

"I'm going to look like the iceberg that sank the *Titanic!*" I protest. "Or like I'm trying to be his twin."

"Great line, but one, direct comments about the *Titanic* at other people, never at yourself, and two, his subconscious will know you're interested because you're dressed similarly."

Of the two of us, she is the successful dater—or at least the only one who's ever *had* a date—so I check out the price tag (twenty bucks) and stick my arms into the sleeves.

I have to admit it looks mostly okay on me. Not as iceberg-y as I thought.

"Voilà!" Liz says, straightening the collar. "Chris the Fabulous!"

It feels different on Friday night though, when we're walking to Lillian's. Trying something new when it's just me and Liz is one thing. People are going to notice I'm dressed up and think it's weird. Even my parents asked if I was going somewhere special when I left the house in this getup.

"Remind me again why I let you talk me into this?" I ask on the way up the steps. My penny loafers are a little loose (at Goodwill, you take what you can get size-wise) and a blister is already starting.

"Because you luuurrvvee Tom Waters, and now he's going to notice you! You know I'm right."

She rings the doorbell, and Lillian's mom ushers us inside and points down a staircase.

"They're in the rumpus room," she says.

"The rumpus room," I whisper, following Liz down. "If I was a housewife serial killer in the fifties, that's where I'd keep my victims."

"Your snark is showing," Liz whispers back. "And I love it!"

Downstairs, all the theater nerds seem present and accounted for. Tom is standing in a corner talking to the actor types. He's wearing his white tux jacket and a skinny tie. He must have had a haircut after school, because it's shorter than it was in bio today, but he's got the usual facial-hair-scruff thing going on. My fingers itch to feel it.

Still, I automatically migrate over to the techie corner, where a game of air hockey is going on. Gordon's leaning against the wall, waiting for a turn. "Dude, you're a Dapper Dan," he exclaims.

"Totally!" Emily Lupine agrees.

I *knew* this was a mistake. They're all wearing black and I feel like a great white walrus next to them.

Tom breaks away from his group to grab a drink from the ice chest and Liz pokes me. "Go!" she hisses. "Make your move."

My kneecaps are tingling as I walk over. I can't tell if that's a good thing or a bad thing.

Tom's fishing around in the ice. "Any Perrier?" I ask.

"I don't think so," he says, grabbing a Coke and straightening up to look at me. He takes in my jacket. If I felt stupid a minute ago, hanging with the tech crew, I feel ten times that now, because the look in his eye is not one of oh-you're-dressed-like-me-now-I-know-you're-interested-let's-go-make-out. It's more of a what-the-hell-am-I-seeing? look.

In the uncomfortable silence, I decide the tingling in my knee-caps is a bad thing.

"Sure we can't get together this weekend to finish the tree? If not, early in the week is good, too. I mean, anytime that's good for you is good for me. I don't have much going on," I babble because he's not saying anything. He's just . . . looking at me.

Liz comes over, thank God. This is not going well.

"Hey, Tom," she says, and then, "Chris, what's up with her?" she asks, pointing to Terilyn Coats, who is wearing her usual mismatched outfit. This time it's a leopard top and a plaid miniskirt over hot-pink leggings.

"She looks like a fabric store threw up on her," I recite as instructed.

"God, Chris, you're such a bitch!" Liz says, playfully slapping my arm. She turns to Tom. "Would you say fabric-store vomit? Or massacre at the Scottish zoo?"

Tom arches an eyebrow. He looks me up and down, then

deliberately unbuttons his own jacket, takes it off, and folds it over one arm.

"I like her style," he says, walking away.

Saturday and Sunday are miserable. I spend them both playing Mordock's Giant by myself. I text Tom four times about the assignment.

I don't hear back from him.

On Monday I talk to him just before the bell rings.

"The poster's due in three days. We have to finish," I tell him.

"It'll get done," he says, and turns to talk to Alex before I can ask him when.

He brushes me off again on Tuesday.

On Wednesday, I grab him in the hall after bio, even though I feel like an idiot creeper for doing it.

"It's almost done, I'll handle it," he says.

He can't draw, and it will definitely look like we waited until the last minute to do it. Which now we have, I guess.

"I am *not* getting a bad grade on this project because of you," I say, my voice louder than I meant it to be.

"I said I'd handle it." His voice is just as loud. He looks over his shoulder at the people flooding out of classrooms on their way to lunch. "Besides, you might catch gay from me," he says, then stalks away.

I stand there for a second, stunned.

Liz comes up behind me and touches my arm. "C'mon, let's go."

I ignore her and run after Tom.

"Wait! Why would you say that?"

He stops to face me. People bump around us.

"It's not cool to make fun of gay people. Especially when you do it to their faces!"

"I wasn't!"

"Yeah, right," he says. "First you say I should carry a little yappy dog in a purse and then you show up at Lillian's dressed like me and acting all . . . whatever! It's like you and your girlfriend went to the stereotype store and cleaned out the merchandise." His voice rises. "And. I. Don't. Appreciate. It."

My first thought is, *Damn!* And then, *Damn Liz's Chris-the-Fabulous idea.*

Tom turns to walk away.

"I swear that's not what I was doing!"

He keeps walking. "It sure seemed like it."

I catch up again. "Really! The truth is . . ."

Oh my God, I can't tell him the truth. Maybe just part of it?

"Liz decided I needed a makeover. She took me shopping and we saw a jacket like yours."

Tom still looks suspicious. "Why would Liz give you a make-over to dress like me?"

Lillian and Alex are heading toward us, and I know we can't

have this conversation right now. "Please. Just let me come over after school. We'll finish the poster and I'll explain."

Even if I'm going to feel like the biggest dork in the world doing it.

He doesn't look happy, but he nods and says, "Be there at four thirty."

Four hours and a bag of Doritos later, I walk up the hill to Tom's. When he answers the door, he doesn't look any happier than he did the last time I saw him. Without a word, he leads me through the house into the kitchen. The poster's laid out flat on the table, a couple of pens and drafting pencils are scattered next to it. His white jacket hangs over the back of a chair, and for some reason, this makes me conscious of the orange Doritos residue on my fingers.

I spent the last couple of hours rehearsing what I was going to say. Now that I'm here all I can come up with is, "Can I have a napkin?"

Instead of answering, he grabs a paper towel from above the sink and hands it to me.

Have you ever noticed how gritty that orange shit is?

"So. Homework first?" I ask.

I get the eyebrow.

Which I take as a no.

I'm pretty sure the term *dead silence* was invented for this exact minute.

I rub away at my fingers until the paper towel finally

disintegrates. I honestly can't remember exactly what I was going to say, and Tom clearly isn't going to help me out.

He leans against the wall, arms folded across his chest.

I feel stupid just standing there, so I ball up what's left of the orangish fibers in my hand, throw them away, and sit down next to the poster.

"Okay. First of all, I only thought of a little poodle when you said you wanted a dog because of the one on your porch. I didn't mean anything by it." I pick up a pen and play with it. "And Lillian's party . . . shit." My voice is shakier than I would like it to be. "Look, I know you won't believe me. Liz didn't, at first, and neither did Gordon, but . . ." I take a deep breath and blow it out.

"I'm gay."

Tom just stares at me for a minute. Like he doesn't believe me. *Here we go again*, I think.

"Let me get this right," he says slowly. There's an expression on his face I can't quite read. "You're gay, so you asked for Perrier at Lil's house?" The left corner of his mouth quirks up. "And you're gay, so you said that mean thing about the way Terilyn dresses?"

I press my lips together. Of course it was stupid.

The right corner of his mouth quirks up to match the left. He closes his eyes for a second. Then he laughs, but it's not a mean laugh. "And you're gay, so you need a white tuxedo jacket?" He pulls his off the chair by its lapels. "Do you think there's a gay handbook or something?"

Laughing again, he makes a big show of shrugging into his coat, smoothing it down, and brushing imaginary dust off the sleeves.

"No," I mumble. "The jacket was because . . ."

He's still laughing when he sits next to me.

"It's a great look," I say. "I mean, you look really . . . amazing in yours."

Tom goes quiet when I say that. He studies me for a minute. I study him right back. There are a few deep gray flecks in his eyes that, for all my previous scrutiny, I somehow never noticed before. The grandfather clock chimes once.

My kneecaps tingle. In a good way, this time.

Tom's the first to move. He grabs a drafting pencil and pulls the poster toward himself.

I shift closer and watch while he sketches a figure at the top of the tree. It has hair that looks remarkably like mine.

"I thought you couldn't draw!" I say.

"I lied." He shrugs his shoulders and adds a dimple to the chin that matches mine. Still focused on the drawing, he says, "I wanted us to do this together."

He keeps sketching. "Something I like about you is that you make dumb jokes in biology. And, I like that you make dumb jokes everywhere else, too." He adds little high-top tennis shoes to my feet. "I like that you dress like you don't care what people think." He draws a hole in one of the shoes. "In fact, I can tell you don't care, and I *really* like that." He tags the figure *Chris* and puts down the pencil. "And now you're telling me you're gay."

"Yes, I'm gay," I say. It feels good to say it. It feels right.

"I don't know if I believe Megars about labels being important," he says, facing me.

I look down at the drawing. Kingdom, phylum, class, order,

family, genus, species, and Chris. I trace the mini me with my finger, then look back at Tom.

It flashes through my mind that I'm actually glad Liz is such an idiot about stereotypes. And I'm glad I'm stupid enough to have gone along with her disastrous idea because it ended with me sitting next to Tom Waters, in this room, and at this moment.

I reach out and touch the scruff growing along his perfectly shaped jaw.

And it feels exactly the way I knew it would.

THE NIGHT OF THE LIVING CREEPER
Stephen Emond

A warning to you, dear reader, this is a terrifying tale, a scary story, a haunting hullaballoo. Should you frighten easily, please turn back now. But for those who can't deny their curiosity, what's so grave that you should shut this book and place it on the shelf, you ask? Why, it's a story about a creeper, of course. There's one amongst us, here in our safe little party, our Halloween party, and amongst our friends, our neighbors, our fellows, yes, one of them . . . is a creeper. Perhaps you and I together can crack this case and figure it out before it's too late and someone gets . . . What's that? What's a creeper? Well. Perhaps you should continue to read after all. By the end of this tail (forgive me for I'm a sucker for a cat pun) we'll come face-to-face with the Creeper. Pay attention, so that you may avoid a bone-chilling encounter with him yourself.

My name is Skittles, and I'm a cat. No, I'm not all the colors of the very tasty rainbow. I'm a black cat. My human is a fan of irony, it would seem, or just bad humor, perhaps. This is my human. For the purpose of this story we'll call her Fairy.

THE LEG OVERLAP *THE PILLOW CUSHION* *THE LEG STRETCH*

There she was on her mom and pop's couch with Superhero while her parents were away, getting a little too close for comfort if you ask me, but it's not my business. I just live here. And her parents, and her brother, but they were away for the weekend and this was just a little get-together, so what's the worst that could happen, right? Other guests, let's see. I could see everyone from right here in my spot near Fairy's bedroom door. There were Fairy and Superhero, nuzzling noses or whatever it is humans do to yell "I'M AVAILABLE FOR MATING." There was Top Half of a Horse talking to Hipster in the kitchen area already piling up with dirty dishes, and they were blowing through snacks and booze they shouldn't be drinking. At the table in the dining room playing a game that led to far too much spontaneous laughter for my taste were Sunflower, Zombie, and Squirrel. They're all girls, and oh. Oh, hello. Yes, petting me right then was Skeleton. Hello, Skeleton. I liked him. Hoped he wasn't the creeper.

Ah, right. The creeper. Well, this was a high school party. There were some beverages flowing that Superhero's older brother managed to snag, hormones rampaging about, and a lack of class, but it was Friday night, what the hell, even I've been known to indulge in some nip and fall asleep with my legs open when it's the weekend. So guards were down, hearts were open, the holidays approached, and it was prime territory for creeping. There was a creeper creeping and there was a fresh young doe, ripe for the kill. I warned you, this is a scary story.

We'll skip most of the party, some of it boring, some of it charming. We'll skip the dancing and the TV watching and the silly pictures and get right to the game because that's where my tale, the haunting ghostly creeper tale, begins.

"Nice guy or bad boy?" Squirrel asked, and sipped from a bottled beer. I should point out, since you were away for this part of the story, that this young vixen was not in a full body anthropomorphized squirrel suit, no. No, she was a sexy squirrel. Why, you ask? Because sexy cats are so played out. That or she didn't want to compete with me. Just sayin'.

"Bad boys," Zombie chimed in, cute yet horrific. Big red framed glasses, messy hair, skin falling off her face. All I got was an orange collar for a costume.

Fun fact: she makes exactly the same face as a confused Labrador.

"Nice guys!" Sunflower said, because what else would a Sunflower say? "Don't you want to be with someone that's your best friend?"

"That's what best friends are for," Squirrel replied. "Guys are for sex." A bold human statement if there ever was one. Really, they were somewhere between being grown and acting grown, these young adult kids. And this was an odd little game, questions and answers, inappropriateness and giggles.

And that's when the gentlemen joined the table. "Guys, sex," they heard, and scurried along like lemmings. Not Superhero, who certainly had sex on the brain already couched up with Fairy, but Top Half of a Horse and Hipster, who each grabbed a chair, ready to hear more of this conversation.

"At your service!" Top Half of a Horse said with a big cheesy grin, and the girls all laughed. He slammed his drink on the table and straddled a chair backward like only the coolest of the cool do, or would if this were a bad nineties romantic comedy. He was the funny one. "What's this game, what are we playing?"

"You don't want to play this one," Squirrel said, dashing him off with her hands but daring, just daring him to play along.

"We're in," Hipster said. But before he was in, he was accosted for his costume, or lack of. "It's a costume, I'm a hipster!"

"Those are your clothes!" Zombie said. "That's exactly what you wore to school today."

"But I'm wearing them ironically now," Hipster said. "Like a hipster would!"

Really, any one of these horned-up gentlemen could be the creeper, but being horned up and flirting, that's not really quite it, that's not exactly creeping. Even Superhero on the couch who at this very second was kissing-but-not-kissing my human the Fairy by covering his mouth with his dirty fingers wasn't necessarily creeping, and Fairy, much to my chagrin, had done nothing to tell him this was not welcome. I'd considered saying something myself but Skeleton was a damned good petter and I wasn't one to stop a good petting.

"All right, boys, next question then," Squirrel said deviously. "Does size matter?"

"*Pass*," Sunflower said with great emphasis.

"Easy. Of course not!" Top Half of a Horse proclaimed, impressed with himself and likely telling the room far too much about himself, but that was the game, I suppose. They laughed. He was pretty funny.

"Is that why you're the top half of a horse?" Squirrel asked and giggled. "Because you're not the bottom half of a horse?"

"Yes, it matters," Fairy called out from the couch. Superhero grinned.

"Actually *really* glad you said that," he said, and I made a note to not sit on his lap.

"But, it's not *all* that matters," Fairy finished, in a way that made me feel a bit embarrassed for her, but I felt that way for most humans, not least of all my human, who often found a way to embarrass herself. My dorky, innocent fairy, who I could more or less guarantee had no idea what she was talking about. If you could see my fuzzy kitty cheeks, I assure you they were blushing.

"And you girls?" Top Half of a Horse asked. "Big deal or no?"

"It doesn't hurt," Squirrel said, adding, "unless it does, I dunno." And they laughed some more.

"Ew," Sunflower added, her eyes closed tight.

The questions went on like this for a while, I'm afraid, and more cheap beer was drunk, and Skeleton continued to not contribute but hung out with me for most of the night, and I wondered if he was the creeper. I mean, it makes sense that the creeper would be quiet. Perhaps he was strategizing, nursing his just one beer, watching the others slip further into silliness, waiting the night out. Or maybe he was just antisocial, or maybe he just realized my fur is quite soft and worthy of extended stroking. He wouldn't be wrong.

"Sex is not a big deal," Squirrel said to Sunflower in regards to something I missed. This game was made for this party, these girls, this age. Sex is not a big deal, she said, yet she'd hardly talked about another subject all night. "It's sex!" she proclaimed obviously. "It's pretty much good in every way."

"You talk a good game," Top Half of a Horse said, "maybe too good a game? I'm having trouble believing all this talk."

"Please, if anyone's a virgin here," Squirrel said dismissively.

"Hey, I'm honest," said Top Half of a Horse. "That one time was pretty enjoyable, I hope to repeat it in the not-too-distant future."

"It is kind of a big deal," Sunflower said. "It is for me, at least. I mean, I'm not a hook-up girl. I'm not an *anything* girl. Some person is going to know every last little detail of your body, you're entrusting them with everything. It's as close as you can possibly get to someone. That's a big deal."

"It's just the human body," Squirrel said, suddenly a biology teacher. "That's nowhere near as close as someone can get, how about your mind? Your day, your routine? Your life? Sex is all external."

"It's probably a bigger deal when you aren't having it," Zombie said, and Sunflower stuck her hand up in the air sheepishly.

"Guilty," Sunflower said. Oh, she was adorable. I know, I'm being catty, but sex is literally nothing to a cat. Don't judge.

"You're in great company," Top Half of a Horse said. "Guilty as well."

Meanwhile, on the couch:

If you wonder why he was only borderline creeping still, it's because Fairy hadn't actually done a thing yet to indicate this was anything but all right. And in fact, yes, she was then rubbing his shoulders. I couldn't even be mad at him as Skeleton was still patting my head an hour on and I'd no intention of stopping him.

Zombie picked up another card. "Catcalls, yes or no?" she asked, and my ears perked. I can't help it, if you were wondering, they just do it on their own.

"I'm seventeen," Sunflower said. "I don't need any fifty-year-old guys saying anything suggestive to me."

"No to catcalls," Zombie said, and placed the card back down.

"Why no?" Squirrel asked, ever the instigator. "It's not hurting anyone."

"Because *no*! Don't argue it!" Zombie said. "At the zoo, you don't feed the animals, and on the street, you don't feed the creepers. You're screwing us all over if you engage them. Anyone who thinks creepers are harmless hasn't been sufficiently creeped. No, no, and another no. Three noes from me."

"Creepers, what's a creeper?" Top Half of a Horse asked.

Well, that was the question, wasn't it? Were you a creeper, Top Half of a Horse? Hiding behind a façade of don't-know?

"Oh, I've been creeped," Squirrel said, surprising exactly no one. "Do you remember this kid, Geoff ... Geoff Something-with-an-L." — — — — — — — — — — — — — — — — ➤

"I need to be more of a pest, is basically what you're saying," Top Half of a Horse said, and Squirrel smiled and pointed, like *now you know the secret.*

"Ugh! See what happens when you feed the creepers?" Sunflower said, crossing her plant-leaf arms.

The Tale of GEOFF Something-with-an-L

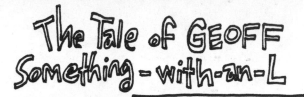

Geoff was this kid I ran into everywhere I went last year of high school.

I don't know how to describe him other than annoying. The brother I never had or wanted.

He'd ask me out every time he saw me, but not to date or be his girlfriend, but more of an "invitation."

He wanted sex. No interest in dating, which is fine since he couldn't get me anyway. He was just horny.

What are you doing tonight?

Come over. My parents aren't home.

Let's hang out already.

I made out with him once and then I had to change up my routine for the rest of the summer.

"Joking!" Top Half of a Horse said. "I'm clearly joking, everything I say is a joke, all right? Moving forward."

"I've got a worse story than that," Zombie said. "Have you ever gotten the Zero-to-Sixty?"

The Zero-to-Sixty

That's when you're sitting with a guy, it's going okay, it's whatever, you're hanging out, talking.

You haven't decided if you like him or not, maybe you'll exchange numbers, see him again sometime, if he plays his cards right.

Then... BAM!

"*Mister bulge,*" Zombie finished. "No warning at all, look who joined the party. I'm like, *where the hell did that thing come from?*"

Sunflower's mouth was agape in shock. Mine would be, too, if that were a thing cats did. "It was still . . . like, inside his pants, right?" she asked, and everyone giggled.

"Thank God, yes," Zombie said. "He sees that I see, he's got some creepy eye contact going. I started laughing. What did he expect? Who's sitting there having a totally normal conversation with a full hard-on? We were talking about winter break plans, for crying out loud. I told him I had to go use the bathroom and he was gone by the time I got out. It was funny but so not funny."

"It's horrible," Squirrel said. "But funny."

"Hang on, I should be taking notes," Top Half of a Horse said, and they all laughed. "Joking, of course, if it needs to be said." Superhero on the couch was beginning to look like a gentleman compared to these creepers.

"It happens," Squirrel said. "I've made out with guys I had no attraction to just because they were nice and I didn't want to be rude."

"I don't think I like these stories," Sunflower said, visibly upset. "I'm nervous enough about going to college. I don't need to hear this."

"Oh, that's exactly why you do need to hear it," Squirrel said. "Recognize game, young sunflower. Avoid the mistakes of your foresisters."

"I feel like I might get crucified here," Top Half of a Horse said, "but, this being Halloween, I do think I should play devil's advocate. Guys get creeped, too, am I right?"

Squirrel, Sunflower, Zombie, and even Fairy on the couch booed this idea.

"He's not incorrect," Super-hero said, ill-advisedly. You were doing so good, bro. "Guys do get creeped on, what about gold diggers? Or all these teacher stories you read in the news. That's creeping."

This guy's more fun than a ball of yarn and about as smart! I kid.

"You spend a lot of time worried about gold diggers, do you?" Squirrel asked, looking at the cheap beer he'd brought.

"Let's not even pretend it's the same thing, okay? You don't need to have a buddy to walk you through the mall parking lot if it's after eight. You don't have to constantly worry about rape."

"Oh, and I thought you were just fine with your catcallers and 'it's just the body,'" Sunflower said.

"Men get raped," Superhero said, and was booed again. Tough crowd. I liked it.

"You can head the discussion next party, all right?" Zombie said. "And I promise to be nothing short of empathetic. But right now these conversation cards are for *girl talk*."

"Now you tell us," Top Half of a Horse said. "I must look like a real ass."

"Can I tell my creeper story?" Fairy asked, sitting up from the couch. "I have one, too, but mine was a long-term, slowly unfolding gradual creep. It was my second boyfriend, sophomore year.

You guys remember Jake. Artsy, smart, good taste in music, read books. We dated for most of that year but he got more and more controlling and obsessive each month. Any time I wanted to break up he'd pull some desperate attention-seeking stunt. He'd make me feel stupid, and I'm not stupid, but he was a lying weasel-faced manipulator. Total long-term creep."

"That's a terrible story, and I'm sorry," Top Half of a Horse said, "but I'm not sure it fits the category of creeping we're developing."

"He was a creeper!" Fairy said. "He lied all the time and used my good nature to get what he wanted. Creepers and liars go hand in hand, buster. Who's with me? All in favor of this weasel being a creeper, say aye."

Hipster agreed immediately. The girls and most of the guys agreed, and eventually the Top Half of a Horse agreed as well. "I told you, I have to play devil's advocate, it's in my nature," he said.

Superhero shook his head. "Jake's your classic phony," he said to Fairy, now sitting normal-sitting-distance away from her. "If you had known me then, he'd have been taken care of a month in, two tops." I'll mention here that Hipster noticeably rolled his eyes at this. Tension! I think I purred.

"All right, I'm gonna get crap for this," Zombie said, "but I think every man is capable of creeping and worse. I'm talking forcing themselves on someone."

"Define *capable*," Superhero said. "Because that's a pretty loaded statement."

"All right. This doesn't go for general creepy behavior, some guys are born with that and some aren't. But guys become imbalanced, chemically, because of their . . ." She trailed off. "And the guy you come to a party with may not be the same guy you leave a party with. I think, in that altered state, guys are capable of some really bad stuff. I've seen it firsthand."

"Well, first, I'm sorry you experienced that, but I still have to disagree," Superhero said. "Any guy can control that, you still have a functioning brain, even if you're not necessarily thinking with it. I think if they can't, it's a much deeper issue than having a penis."

"That brings up an issue, here's a question," Top Half of a Horse said. "So if every girl has these admittedly awful creeper stories, can any guy here admit to being a creeper? Even one time? I mean, it stands to reason that the creepers are out there, and we are four guys at this party. Is anyone a creeper? I'll go first—I don't think I am. At least I'd hope I'm not, and if I am, someone tell me, please. You guys?"

Hipster shook his head. "Absolutely not. I could point one out in a crowd but I am assuredly not one myself."

"Not me," Skeleton mumbled. Good for you, Skeleton, contributing and all. He drank from his beer.

"Not me," Superhero said. "I've never needed to creep."

"Come on," Hipster said to this. "You're going to tell us you're not a creeper? That whole Jake story was about manipulation. If manipulation is part of this broadening definition of creeping, then you're a creeper."

"Whoa, unprovoked attack, hello," Superhero said. "If I'm a creeper for manipulation, then you're all creepers, too, and essentially every guy throughout history is a creeper also. I say manipulation gets taken out of the definition. It's in the DNA of every relationship from the dawn of time. I mean, the whole point of courtship is to woo some impressionable, hopefully single female to your side. You say whatever's gonna work, you make yourself look a little better than you probably are. It's called flirting, and everyone does it."

"Flirting and lying are very different," Hipster said. "Let's draw a clear line there."

"You're both making sense," Top Half of a Horse mediated. "I'm not disagreeing with any of this."

Superhero and Fairy made their way sloppily to the table, and Skeleton left me, too, to join the table. It's noteworthy to mention that Fairy chose a seat clear across the table from the Superhero she couldn't get close enough to just moments earlier. I jumped on the kitchen counter for a better view.

"What's the difference between someone you might label a 'player' and any other guy in the room, besides success rate?" Superhero asked, passionate on his subject. "What's an opening line? What's your 'move'? Hell, what about people who meet online? Guys and girls, everything they say online is BS. Everyone's a world-traveling philosophical-genius health nut who can only take a picture from one angle. People lie to get what they want, a boyfriend or girlfriend, or just to get laid. Is everyone online a creeper, too?"

"It's highly likely," Squirrel said.

"I don't manipulate," Hipster said definitively, sticking to his guns. "Honestly. If a girl doesn't like me for exactly who I am, I don't see the point in lying to make her like me. Let's face it, that's never going to work out anyway. I'd rather be single than putting on some façade all day. I may be alone at a party, sad as that is. Yes, my existence is sad, but. When I do find someone you can be sure as hell our relationship will build off of honesty and no bull. It'll take me longer to get there but I'm gonna have something that's real."

"Aw," Sunflower said.

"No lying. He gets it," Fairy said.

"I get it because I'm smart and great minds think alike," Hipster said with a wink.

"That's good, I like that," Top Half of a Horse said, continuing to play game-show host for whatever this discussion had spiraled into. "You raise a good point."

"Absolutely false," Superhero said. "I'll be the bad guy, but I'm still the honest one. You want to know what you are? I've got a lot of thoughts on this, so indulge me for a second. I can't stand phonies.

"You're the guy that judges people for liking horror movies and MMA and stuff. Or rap lyrics. Like one of those who think, 'How can anyone listen to that violent hateful stuff? How can anyone watch those dark movies, what disturbed mind enjoys that?' And you know what? These are the friggin' Boy Scout leaders and clergymen who molest kids, these are the religious kooks that condemn everything on the face of the earth and go home and beat their wives, the politicians who cheat and lie and spread hypocrisy. People so scared to acknowledge any darkness in human nature, which is probably a good fifty percent of our molecular makeup

if we're honest. You think worse things than anyone, your brains are full of hellish nightmare thoughts, but your inability to indulge in let alone accept that a dark side even exists at all makes you the most horrifying thing on the planet. You ignore a whole side of yourself and let it fester, and you gotta take out your aggression on everyone else just doing their thing and being happy. You guys are the absolute worst. No offense. I'm not even mad right now, I'm just telling it like it is, because I've encountered this before. At least I'm honest in what I want, manipulation or not."

"Honesty is a great word, man, but not every girl is going to respect that kind of honesty," Hipster said, not missing a beat. Brave boy. Superhero could take him in a fight in three seconds flat, if I wagered a guess. "I'm just saying, manipulation might be at the root of everything but no one *has* to manipulate or be manipulated," he said. "I mean, people have choices, they can go with the nice guy, even if he isn't overbearing and in your face and *bam, here it is*." Hipster actually pointed to his crotch.

"Oh, Jesus," Superhero said, exasperated.

"Can I say something?" our shy little Skeleton asked. "These are kind of all fallacies. Nice guys and bad boys, you know. Neither one is real. The nice guys are jerks all the time, the bad boys can be not bad at all. And vice versa. It's called being a person. Three-dimensional and everything. With an actual history, and reasons for the way they do things, their own unique beliefs and views. I mean, I know people have tendencies, and it's not that hard to put everyone in a box. Maybe we even have to, just to deal with the wealth of options and information in the world. But. I mean, it's not a great argument settler, but everyone's at least a little right and a little wrong."

"I think he just called you a creeper," Hipster said to Superhero, and everyone laughed.

Really, any one of these guys could have been a creeper. That's the difficulty with this sort of thing. Any one of them could have been creeping, looking to get a lady's defenses down and take what they want. Any one of them could have been a genuinely nice friendly fellow. Any one of them could have been sad and lovelorn, or content to be single, or maybe even taken already. It's not like they make T-shirts for the loud and proud creeper. But tonight, yes, one of these men was creeping.

Let's recap.

There's Hipster. He's argumentative. I think he's got a thing for Fairy. But overall he seems positive and well-mannered, he's open with his thoughts and feelings.

Superhero is aggressive, he expects things, he's used to getting his way. He flies off the handle easily, he's opinionated, but has he crossed any lines? Would he?

The Top Half of a Horse is certainly outgoing and gets all the girls laughing. Is he mediating controversy or is he stirring the pot? He can be self-effacing. What are his issues with himself?

Then there's Skeleton. Quiet. Is he brooding, is he just shy? Hard to get a grip on this one. He likes cats, that's a plus on any young man's scorecard. And he had a good strong point regarding individuality amid the arguments.

Maybe if we could go back in history, really get to know these men, maybe then it'd all be a little more clear. If we knew that the Top Half of a Horse came from a broken home, that he was hit as a child, or that Skeleton was in fact homosexual, or if we knew that Hipster was a virgin or that Superhero had four sisters. Maybe if we had these details we'd be able to say, "Aha, this one here is a bona fide creeper!"

But we don't have those details. In fact, the ones I just told you I made up on the spot, being a clever kitty and story spinner myself. As for motivations, personal histories, what's going on in that mind we can't see or read . . . we never know those details in real life, not when we first meet someone, and sometimes not for long after. We can go pretty far along on just intuition and trust.

"Well, I think I'm gonna get outta here," the Top Half of a Horse said, standing up from the table and having a stretch. "Thank you, all. This has been a . . . What's it been? It's been a philosophical, engaging, informative, and eye-opening evening. Does that sum it up?"

"Stay!" Sunflower called out.

"I can't, I can't," Top Half of a Horse said. "I've got a bottom half somewhere out there painting the town red, I gotta track it down."

But seriously, he's the slobbering mastiff of comedy.

Hipster got up next and brought his dishes to the kitchen.

"I'm out, too," Squirrel said. "I'm parked down the street. Walk me to my car?"

"Absolutely, and I'd walk you out of the mall, too," Top Half of a Horse said.

"I guess that's a wrap, then. We didn't even get to the next card," Zombie said, lifting a card out of the box. "In the bedroom with your lover—lights on or off?"

"Next time, you undead provocateur," Superhero said, standing up himself. "That'll give me time to prepare a whole dissertation, really do my research. I'm not getting booed again."

Skeleton and Sunflower both stood up and everyone got their coats on and said their good-byes, did their hugging thing, and opened the door. I sat on that counter looking adorable, I'll tell you, and Hipster looked straight at me without even a smile. He stepped back out of the kitchen, cleaning a glass with a towel still.

"Your parents are out for a while, right? Can I crash on your couch?" he asked. "Feeling a little tipsy, total lightweight. I'll help you clean up."

"Yeah, sure," sweet trusting Fairy said, stepping into her bedroom. I hopped off the counter and rushed past Hipster's feet to my human. She pulled her arms in through the straps that held her wings in place and put the wings down on the bed. Hipster was faster than me, into her room, and he put his hand over her shoulder.

"I was glad you got him off you," Hipster said, speaking of Superhero. "Dude's really aggressive. In all honesty, I'm not a fan. You could probably tell from all the banter. Dude's not exactly an intellectual giant, he's actually kind of fun to argue with." Fairy didn't have many options on where to go, so she slowly turned around, and Hipster rested his hand on her shoulder as long as he could. Now she was facing him directly, barely a breath's space between them. "I always liked you," he said. He laughed nervously.

I meowed, my only method of spontaneous communication.

I enjoy this kid like I enjoy having my butt petted, which is to say not at all.

"Skittles," Fairy said, and moved her head around Hipster's shoulder to look at me. "I have to feed Skittles." Yes, yes, human, you need to feed your cat. And get that creeping Hipster out of here.

"You need any help?" he asked, following her like a shadow, leaving barely a space between them still. He knew, like Superhero knew when he sat at the table, that his game was as good as over if she left his side.

"I got it," Fairy said, and we went back into the kitchen.

"All right," Hipster said, stopping in the space outside the kitchen and slowly starting to take off his left shoe. Fairy turned and saw the action.

"Maybe we should call it a night," Fairy said, pouring with a shaky hand, bits of dry food bouncing back out of my bowl. "I'm kinda tired after the whole party." Good girl, stick to your guns.

"You sure?" Hipster asked, pausing in his movements and lowering his foot. He walked closer. "Can I still . . . or call it a night, like you want me to leave?"

Fairy placed my dish on the ground. I took a bite but I wasn't hungry, go figure. That was a first for me. I turned my head to look at Hipster, standing in the kitchen doorframe, blocking her in. I was prepared to pee on the floor, if needed.

"You should go," Fairy said. I'd have preferred she told him *"Out!"* in no uncertain terms, like I've heard so many times. You've been a *bad cat.*

"I mean, we don't have to—" Hipster started.

"Get out," Fairy said, assertive this time, and pointed. "The door's right there."

"Sorry, leaving," Hipster said, backing up and grabbing his coat. He swung his coat on as fast as he could open the door. "See you around."

"Night," Fairy said after the door slammed shut, with an annoyed wave of hand.

We both walked to the door and Fairy locked it and sat down beside me. She took a deep breath, and exhaled. She petted me on the head and I purred. I was happy. "What's going on with you?" she asked in her high-pitched cat-conversing voice, and scratched behind my ears. "Huh, little guy? Weren't you going to tell me he was a creeper? We don't let creepers in our home."

You mean we could have chased him off with a broom earlier? If I'd only known.

You know, that dry food was starting to sound good.

MAKESHIFT

Kekla Magoon

The windows in our new apartment have no curtains. Whoever lived here before us left rolls of wrapping paper to cover them. One edge of the paper is taped to the upper lip of the frame with X's of duct tape, then the tube has been simply dropped and unfurled. It's holiday paper. In the living room, one window wears a sheet of rosy grinning Santas; the other, a poinsettia theme of red, green, and white. In the room that will be mine, it's silver and gold menorahs on glistening black. Jewish roommate? Crisis of faith? Random grab out of the bargain bin? These are the things I wonder as I unfold my air mattress and locate the power outlets.

Then I sit among my few boxes and my suitcase and stare at that Hanukkah "curtain" all afternoon. This is how we live now. We have nothing.

Protruding nails occupy the walls on either side of each window frame, halfway up. You can pick up the wrapping paper tube from the floor, roll it up to there, and rest it on the nails. Some weirdo's idea of raising the blinds, I guess.

In my real house, the blinds had a remote control. You pushed a button and they'd slide up and down easily. I had three windows in that room.

Finally, I do it. Raise the non-curtains—the wrapping paper / nail system turns out to be functional enough—and gaze out at my new street: 138th Street. Harlem, New York.

It's relatively quiet down there, in the only way it can ever be quiet in the heart of the city, as far as I can tell: with the ambient hum of the rest of Manhattan hovering somewhere behind everything.

It must be garbage day; mounds of huge black plastic bags line the curbs. A group of kids walking down the street rearrange themselves from a pod into single file to dodge the trash piles. The kids look several years younger than me, middle school maybe, walking and joking. Tomorrow I'll also have to walk. It's six blocks to my new school. I still can't believe any of this is happening. It doesn't feel real.

Mom comes in. "Kayse, I need you to . . ." she starts. Stops. Glances around. "What have you been doing in here? I thought you were unpacking."

The smell of Lysol wafts at me from the yellow gloves on her hands. I drag my gaze from the window to look at her, though there's nothing to say. I don't know what good unpacking is going to do me anyway. It's not like I have any furniture.

Mom shakes her head. "Baby, go down to the bodega and grab us some more paper towels." Mom thrusts two five-dollar bills into my hand. She glances around the room. "You haven't even cracked a box."

"What's a bodega?"

Mom sighs. "The corner store."

"Which corner?"

She places her forearms on my shoulders, keeping the Lysol gloves aloft, and walks me to my window. She points.

My face scrunches. "That place?" The greasy-looking storefront has boxes of cereal and stuffing mixes in the window, their labels faded to a common yellow-beige by too much time in the sun through the glass. "It looks gross."

"And when you get back," Mom says with a last-warning glare, "you are going to clean that bathroom."

"I have to unpack," I grumble.

"Huh. Your unpacking looks like a whole lotta nothing right now." She leans in and kisses the side of my face. Fast, before I can duck away. Annoying.

My elbow bumps her chest as I jerk away from the affection. She winces slightly. Her ribs are still sore. Her cheek, still bruised along the jawline. A slight stab of guilt pierces me. She's working hard, through the pain, to get this place ready for us, and I'm just sitting here.

"Fine," I say. "I'm not peeing in there until it's scrubbed down anyway." I kind of have to pee, now that I've said it. But it's okay. I can hold it in.

Mom's tender expression says she wants to touch me, or would, but for the Lysol gloves. It's hard to hate her when she looks so damn pathetic. Her cheek is swollen, red-purple. The bruise has a life of its own. I have a whole conversation in my head with it, every minute. I'd rather look at the other side of Mom's face, but it seems like the hurt side is always pointing toward me.

It's temporary, I remind myself. *We'll only be here a little while.* He's going to have to pay her alimony, eventually. Or child support. He has to, right? They were married my whole life. He's my dad, for Christ's sake.

Maybe, on account of my room decor, I should start saying something Jewish instead. For menorah's sake? I have no idea.

I should know some Jewish sayings, really. My two best friends, Hannah and Emma, are Jewish. But we've never actually talked about it. Them being Jewish, or me being half black. We're always just ourselves together.

Mom is black and Dad is white, just like my biological father, who disappeared soon after I was born. Dad's only slightly less of a deadbeat human than that guy, as it turns out. One who took fifteen years to show his true colors, not fifteen months. I don't know which is worse now: hating the father I never knew or hating the one I always loved.

"How could he do this to us?" I didn't mean to say it out loud. Talk of Dad is taboo right now. Neither of us has mentioned him once in the week since we left home.

Mom shifts her jaw. The bruise blinks between angry and sad. "Paper towels, please, honey."

In the short walk to the corner, all the faces that I pass are medium-skinned or darker. Since we arrived in Harlem, I've seen very few people as light-skinned as Mom even, and fewer who are as light-skinned as me.

I never felt very black in Connecticut, but I feel pretty white here. I'm both, I guess. And neither. This is not the most confusing thing of the past few days, but not the least either. Walking in this new place makes me feel like I'm also walking in new skin.

Between my building and the bodega, there are several other apartment buildings, a tiny take-out taco place, and a shoeshine / watch repair stand. There is a bone-thin, rough-bearded guy lurking on the curb in front of the shoeshine spot. He leers creepily at me.

"Beautiful, blanca," he says, as soon as I am in earshot.

I'm not white, I want to shout at him. The impulse rises up so strongly, it shocks me into staying silent. Here I am, among all these other black people, and yet I clearly don't belong.

"Looking sexy tonight, mamí" he adds, and I stick to my guns, saying nothing. Jerks who hit on you on the street don't deserve the time of day as far as I'm concerned. I beeline for the bodega door, keeping to the far side of the sidewalk.

He steps to the middle. Too close for comfort. "What?" he says. "You don't like to talk to people? You think you're too good for a guy like me?" He throws his arms out to the sides, like a scarecrow in ragged but clean-looking clothes.

I slip through the door, listen to the jangle of bells as it closes behind me. I can still hear his voice: "You would look so much prettier with a smile on that face, blanca."

*B*lanca. White girl. The word follows me home, a shadow I can't shake. Just like the scarecrow guy's gaze on me. Except it's not on me. It's *in* me. Somehow.

"I need you to go to the bodega again," Mom says, the second I walk into the apartment. "I forgot to buy butter earlier."

"How could you forget to buy butter?" I snap. As if Mom is supposed to be perfect or something. As if we would never have run out of butter if we were back home.

"Lay off me, Kaysandra," Mom groans. "Please?" The bruise argues her point even more loudly. A compelling witness to everything wrong with us.

I force myself to look away from her cheek, meet her eyes. That's when I remember: the bruise is a distraction from the truth of her. Mom can win anything with her strong, quiet gaze. It's a force field.

"It's up to you," she says finally. "We can just have biscuits without butter."

I don't know how to tell her I don't want to go back down there while that guy is lurking around.

Mom doesn't even like biscuits that much. I know she's baking them to make the house smell good. To make it feel like home. To cover the scent of the ache that lingers around us.

I'm the one who likes biscuits. Mom bakes to take care of me, even though she's annoyed at me for this attitude I can't seem to drop. It's what she did when I was little, like she's trying to take us back to those days when every wound went away with a Strawberry Shortcake Band-Aid and a kiss.

It's been a long time since Mom fixed anything for me. It's usually Dad I look to for comfort.

I spin toward the door. "Fine, whatever."

Even from the dim, smudge-walled hallway, I can smell the

fresh dough baking. The biscuits will be nothing without butter. Even sadder than we are.

I'm more nervous this time, approaching the store.

"Back so soon, mamí? Still looking fine," says the scarecrow guy, now smoking the stub of a thin hand-rolled cigarette.

I ignore him. It feels right, like last time.

"You come back to see me? I'm waitin' for that smile."

Approaching the store from the other direction is a girl about my age. She wears tights and a short skirt and a top that cleaves low. Across her chest, a wide gold script necklace says MANNIE. We both pause, stepping aside to let a couple of young kids race out of the bodega. The door's bell jangles and their footsteps scrape the concrete sidewalk. Their laughter is a bursting, lively thing.

I'm stopped in front of the smoking guy, who's full of talk. "What, you still don't wanna make friends?" he leans in. "'S all right. You go on, be your tight-ass self. 'S cool."

"Jesus, Carl. Lay off her," Mannie snaps from the other side of the doorway. "Can't you see she ain't from around here? Save your bullshit for someone who's got a shovel."

"Woo!" Carl hoots. "Someone's sassy today."

Mannie rolls her eyes and whips past me as we enter the bodega. Over her shoulder she tells me, "These guys. They don't mean nothin' by it. You just gotta put 'em in their place, you know?"

I *don't* know. I've walked by Carl several times now, and I'm

still kind of freaked by him. He didn't try to grab me or anything.
But he could.

"It's too weird," I admit.

Mannie waves a hand. "They think they're being friendly."

"I guess," I answer, but the icky feeling remains.

"You lost?" Mannie asks. "Where you tryin' to get to?"

"I'm not lost."

"Oh." She shrugs. "We don't get many white girls around here."

"I'm not white." I blurt it out, in spite of myself. I grab one cold
box of butter and hold it tight in my hand. I never cared before
that people often assume I'm white. I never bothered to correct
them. I'm as much white as black, underneath—half and half. I
always have been. It's fresh and unsettling, the urge to erase that
part of me.

Mannie looks closer. "Oh, yeah, okay. I guess." Like it's up to
her to decide if I have any black in me. I'm tempted to tell her, *Let
me go get my mom; that'll clear it up for you.* But I just pay for my
butter and head toward the door. It'll be worth it in a minute,
I remind myself, imagining the taste of hot biscuits.

"See you around," Mannie says as I go.

"Sure." I force myself to smile at her, though nothing in me
feels like smiling.

Carl sits silent as I pass by him this time. The silence isn't
empty. I know he is watching me go.

Our kitchen is spare, like the rest of the place. We have one
small shaker jar of Italian seasoning. Mom says it can go on

everything. We have one frying pan, one saucepan, one foil tray for baking in the oven. Two plates, two glasses, two spoons, two forks. One knife, which we pass between us.

We have one wooden folding chair and one threadbare armchair with an ottoman. I tuck myself into the armchair while Mom perches on the edge of the folding chair. The ottoman becomes a makeshift table.

Mom shifts forward slightly and the air splits with the sound of splintering wood. The hinge holding the right chair leg together is suddenly loose, and the seat begins sagging, off-kilter.

"Shit," Mom says. I don't know if I've ever heard her curse before. She stands and kicks the wooden chair across the room. It clatters against the wall. "Fucking shit." She stands in the center of the near-empty space, fist against her forehead, fork sticking out from it like a unicorn horn.

"We're going to go home, aren't we?" I ask. "Eventually?"

Mom picks up the plates. She hands me mine and sits down in its place on the ottoman. We are closer now, plates on our knees. "No, baby. We can't go home."

"He's my dad," I insist. "Even if you get divorced, I could still live at home part of the time."

"He can't have you without me," Mom says. "I won't let him. Especially after . . ."

"He's my dad," I remind her again. And I miss him, which I won't say out loud. And my house, and my room and my friends.

"He's not really your dad," she says. "That's the only saving grace in all of this."

I hate her for saying it. "But he adopted me."

"Not legally," she says. "Thank God."

This is news to me. I am fatherless, at least on paper. The truth hits me like a rubber stamp. Ink across my forehead.

Fatherless.

I can feel it in the air, the absence of him, but I can't let myself really breathe it in yet.

"You told me he adopted me." All this time, I thought he wanted me. I thought I belonged to him, like I belonged to Mom.

"He wanted you to know he loved you. So you would feel at home."

"But it was a lie?"

"Oh, honey."

Fatherless. I start to write poetry in my head about it. It doesn't rhyme. The cracks in the foundation beneath my feet spread, like fingers outstretched. We have nothing left, and the earth is still quaking.

"Who's my real father?" I ask. I've never needed to know before—I had a dad. "Do you even know?"

"Of course I do," Mom says. "Who do you think I am?"

"I thought you were my mother," I say. "But I've been wrong before."

Mom looks at me. The bruise is all I see. It seems so much bigger than it was a minute ago, and yellow around the edges. I wonder, not for the first time, about the wounds that don't show.

"Dad couldn't adopt you, because your biological father wouldn't give up his parental rights," Mom said. "I have no idea why."

I imagine myself, a newborn. Two fathers fighting for me. Wanting me.

"Why don't you just ask Dad for some money?" I say. "Tell him it's for me."

"He's not going to give us money," Mom says. "We left him."

"*You* left him," I protest. "Not me. He loves me." I stop short of saying: *and he wouldn't want me living in a place without furniture or curtains.*

Mom nods. "Yes, he loves you very much," she says.

"He would never hurt me." He wouldn't, but I know she's afraid of it. I can tell.

Mom pushes her food around the plate. "He would never want to hurt you," she says after a while.

"Right. See?" It's not the same as what I said. I know it's not. But I smile anyway, as if she has agreed with me.

"I gravitate toward possessive, angry men," Mom says. "Apparently."

"Dad's not angry," I object, thinking of his near-constant smile, his laugh. His arms going around my shoulders to comfort me.

Mom looks at me. Some kind of knowledge arcs through her gaze, moving from her to me slowly. "He fooled me for a long time, too."

"You always say it's best to forgive people," I say. "Why couldn't you give him another chance?" Now that the lid is off, the words will not stop. Kernels of truth, bursting. A thousand questions.

"I gave him lots of chances," Mom says. "You have no idea."

"It happened one time," I insist. She says he smacked her across the face and stepped on her ribs. I can hardly believe it of him. "I'm sure he didn't mean it."

The bruise is static—purple and present. "I don't expect you to understand," Mom says. She takes up our plates and walks to the kitchen.

We have a half bottle of detergent and one small square sponge. I look at it and I see myself washing things over and over. We have so few dishes; they will never be clean.

Mom comes into the doorway. Watches me scrub. "It starts with words," she says.

I pretend I didn't hear. Scrub for a while, then nudge the faucet off with the side of my palm. "What?"

"He only hit me once," Mom says. "But there are lots of ways to hurt someone. Ways to make a person feel small."

I don't understand this. Even though I don't turn around, over my shoulder I can feel the strength of her stare. Mom may not be a very large woman, but she's entirely the opposite of small.

All my life I thought we were safe. I thought *I* was safe. Our yard had a fence and our windows had burglar alarms.

Now we have Santas, poinsettias, menorahs. Not exactly protection.

Down on the corner somewhere, Carl is sitting. Smoking. I wonder if he has forgotten all about me in favor of someone else who walked by, or if his mind keeps drifting back to me, to that "white" girl who came to the store twice in a row and refused to smile.

Without Dad, this one bedroom walk-up on a gritty block is all we can afford. I have my air mattress in the bedroom and Mom will sleep in The Chair. We'll get a couch soon, she says, and then she'll sleep on that.

Mom grew up in Harlem, so she knows what a bodega is, and that the scratching sound in the walls is mice, and that the banging on the hallway wall is most likely just a drunken neighbor.

In Connecticut we had occasional drunken neighbors, too. They'd fight out on their porches, staggering around in the darkness. Probably thinking nobody could hear. It was never very scary. Never came close. We had mice one summer, but they stayed in the garage. Country mice display that kind of courtesy.

Here in the city, everything is in your face. Back home, the dangerous or dirty things always existed outside a certain circle, beyond the edge of our house, our yard, our town.

I was wrong about that, though. I should have been scared, I guess. I just didn't know it. *This neighborhood is perfectly safe,* Mom said when we arrived. *There's nothing to worry about here, okay?*

I didn't believe her. Still don't. The things that were once safe aren't safe anymore. The circle has grown much smaller.

Mom putters around the kitchen while I finally scrub down the bathroom. I wear the yellow gloves and fan the Lysol fumes out the sliver of window with an old magazine. I hear her clattering pans in there, cooking again. Making my lunch for tomorrow, I suppose. Like she used to.

I wonder if she really thinks it could be that easy to rewind ourselves to a place of less distance. I wonder if it would be okay, now, to let her wrap her arms around me, or kiss my face without my flinching away. If anything would become better. I wonder if she'll press a heart into my sandwich out of M&Ms, and I wonder when our *I love you*'s started to be so silent.

I'll go to a new school tomorrow, with my lunch in a brown paper bag. I'll keep my head down, move through the day at a distance. I've never been the new girl, and I don't want to be now. I want to go unnoticed, be a shadow in the back of the room. *It's only for a while*, I keep telling myself. *We must be going home soon.* It's too much to imagine this as our forever.

A Dad-less forever.

In my old school everyone knew who my parents were. Tomorrow, I'll be the out-of-place, almost-white girl swimming in a sea of dark brown. Will people assume I'm white? Of course they will. I feel sick to my stomach. Because I'm not. *I'm not.*

All this time, I thought the color of my skin didn't really make a difference. I used to think of myself as just myself.

It matters, now, being black, and I don't know why. I don't even look it. I barely feel it.

The bathroom mirror holds no answer. This has always been my skin, yet somehow "black" never seemed part of the surface of me.

I remember the first time someone told me *"You're lucky to be so light."* Less baggage, in the world's eyes. But then in the next breath they try to tell you that how you look doesn't matter. It's all about who you are underneath.

Half black, half white. It's been a current running under

everything my whole life. Tomorrow, will they ask me or just stare at me while they try to figure it out? When they call me blanca, will I have to scream out, *I'm not!* I'm not like him. Not like either of them—not Dad or my real father. Not at all.

Not the one who hits.

Not the one who leaves.

I kneel on the bathroom floor. It's the Lysol fumes. They're making me queasy. That fucking tiny window. I fan the magazine, but it isn't enough. My hands grope the tile, knees knocking the toilet rim. Scramble up, until my face finds the two-inch gap between pane and frame. Breathe Harlem night air, clean and cool and the opposite of silent.

Music pulses at me from somewhere. A distant siren whirls. Tires frisk along pavement as the wind disturbs the leaves below the window.

"Honey?" Mom calls. Maybe she hears me crying.

Mom appears in the bathroom doorway, a dishtowel on her arm and a spatula in her hand. I don't mean to look, it just happens. But I turn away quickly, stare out the slim window opening at the lights in all the buildings.

"I'm fine," I choke out. "I breathed in fumes."

"Come out of the bathroom," she says. "Let it air out for a few minutes."

When I turn around, she's already gone, and I'm grateful. I avoid glancing in the mirror this time.

How things look isn't important. It's how things are that matters. Dad looks like a great, upstanding guy. Chairman of the corporate board, with a perfect haircut.

Dad didn't change overnight. He's always been a friendly guy with a big laugh . . . and an abuser, too, I guess. I've always been a half-black girl who looks all white.

Back in my room, I lower the menorah-covered "curtain." It's so dark out. That never mattered at home, but here I don't know who might be out there looking in. We're four stories up, I know, but the city is nothing but eyes. The wrapping paper tube thumps to the floor with a light bounce and the paper crinkles like static.

The curtains strike me as less silly now, more fragile. One little tear, and everyone would be able to look inside. A fraction of a millimeter of paper between me and the whole world witnessing the fallout after all that has gone wrong.

No way to put it off any longer. I slice open my boxes—consider me unpacked. In the haste to pack, I managed to remember to bring along a few books. I take one out to The Chair and curl up, trying to lose myself in an adventure novel.

Mom moves around in the kitchen, sautéing inexpensive meat and humming "You Don't Own Me." The scent of Italian seasoning and oil fills the air. It blankets me, which I know is her intention. Simple. Enticing. The flavor of home.

Home isn't what it used to be either, though—or what I always thought it was. It's something unfamiliar and new. *It's only temporary.* My lie to myself. This is how we live now.

Pulling myself back out of my book isn't easy. To raise my eyes and look around our new place—so spare, so naked—and try to think of it as home. In the kitchen, Mom pauses her stirring. She tips her head toward me, like she knows what I am thinking—that I wish I could face the world like she does, unafraid.

I have to believe it'll be okay somehow. We might have been hit, but we have not been shattered. We can rewind. There can be Strawberry Shortcake Band-Aids again, and M&M hearts, and laughter.

The book folds easily over the arm of the chair, holding my place. Mom has bought a value-size package of brown paper lunch bags. They're up in the cabinet over the fridge. I slice into the shrink wrap, shake one bag open, put it on the counter. Ready.

Mom touches my face, in the place where the bruise is on her own face. Like a mirror.

It's only temporary. The bruise. The fear. The dent in our force field. The world outside doesn't matter. Tomorrow doesn't matter. Mom is here, and that's more than nothing. For tonight it's just the two of us, inside this wrapping paper bubble.

THINGS YOU GET OVER, THINGS YOU DON'T

Jason Schmidt

PART ONE

Here was a thing Caleb learned about school shootings: a lot of the people who get shot end up surviving. Caleb had looked it up on the Internet, and was surprised to find out that, in most cases, the survivors outnumbered the dead. Evidently, with modern medical technology—and depending on where the school was in proximity to the nearest hospital or whatever—killing someone with a gun was a lot harder than they made it look on TV. Of course, it was the dead people who mostly got talked about afterward; the dead kids in particular. Dead teachers got some play if they did something heroic. Otherwise there was a weird undercurrent of resentment in how the dead teachers were talked about. Like people thought a teacher who got killed without doing something totally Chuck Norris hadn't really earned his or her $40K a year plus benefits. Caleb thought that was unfair. Because, for one thing, if the dead teachers had owed it to the world to die heroically, why did the surviving teachers seem to get a pass? Maybe people were just afraid to criticize someone to their face while they were still alive.

L isa and Caleb had been together for about six months when the shooting started. She was on the rebound when they got together. She'd been with a guy named Phil Young since they were all freshmen, and everyone had sort of assumed Lisa and Phil were going to get married someday. Because it was hard not to have an opinion about high school students who stayed together for more than a few months. Some people called them PhiLisa, like one of those celebrity duos. Caleb himself had been something of a fan, though he didn't know either of them personally until he and Lisa hooked up.

Phil and Lisa, as a couple, had been boring in a way that Caleb found vaguely exotic. Lincoln High School had a huge attendance area; Caleb was from the part where people had bad teeth, diabetes, and funny stories about getting mauled by pit bulls. Phil and Lisa were from not-that-part, and it showed. Phil was six feet tall, and casually athletic. He had short brown hair, and a healthy, if decidedly Anglo-Saxon, complexion. His clothing was nothing special: loose jeans, oxford-cloth button-down shirts, and inexpensive brand-name basketball shoes. But it all had a startling vibrancy to it. Caleb had noticed the same phenomenon in German exchange students.

Caleb thought Phil had the air of a guy who'd go to college and get a professional degree—like a master's in journalism, or business. Maybe a law degree. Phil could do or be anything he wanted in later life. He came from a perfect family. And there'd never be any dirt to dig up on Phil. He seemed to lack the imagination to do bad things. He was the kind of guy who could grow up to be president someday.

Lisa was more or less the girl version of Phil: tallish, medium build, medium-length light-brown hair with blond highlights. Varsity volleyball. She favored knee-length skirts and fitted tops, but sometimes she went with jeans, sneakers, and a T-shirt. Every once in a while she'd come to school wearing thick plastic-framed nerd glasses, which always knocked Caleb for a loop. He figured she was also bound for professional school, though maybe something the tiniest bit more granola than Phil; a master's in social work, or a law degree she'd take to a legal aid organization. Or maybe she'd get married, get a Realtor's license, and be one of those women. She was like a mannequin. A blank slate. Hang any outfit on her, she could be anything—but she'd always be the rich, smart, hot version of whatever she was. Caleb wondered what it must be like to be with someone so unwrought—someone who could be all things, or nothing. Sometimes he thought maybe, if he went away to college, he could reinvent himself and find out: pass for a Phil; score himself a Lisa.

As it worked out, he didn't have to wait that long. Lisa and Phil broke up early senior year. The story around school was that they realized they were too young to be tied down like that. Which made sense, but Caleb couldn't help being a little disappointed. He'd lost his virginity to a college girl at a kegger freshman year, and he'd been on a fairly steady roll since then, but he'd never had a regular girlfriend. Phil and Lisa had been his proxy couple, and their breakup made him question whether anyone could be truly happy in a committed relationship.

A week after her breakup with Phil, Lisa showed up at a barn party in her nerd glasses, and Caleb was pretty much helpless. He chatted her up in the cool-off area all night, between bouts of dancing and trying to pound enough ephedrine to get a buzz going. When the party started to wind down, around three in the morning, she asked him to drive her home.

"My parents are out of town," she said as soon as they were outside, in the quiet night air.

Her room was different than he'd thought it would be. It was definitely a rich girl's room, but it was also more serious than he'd expected. Dark, heavy bedspread. Antiques. Lots of books. The posters on her walls were for theaters and museums, rather than the boy bands and chick flicks he'd imagined. When she let him get past second base he decided to bring his A game, so he went down and did the whole alphabet-with-his-tongue thing. It worked like a charm, and after she came he didn't press for more—he just held her while she shivered, and her breathing slowed.

"Phil would never do this," she said, after a while. Which should have been tacky—bringing up another guy right then—except that it was also exactly what Caleb wanted to hear. He imagined three years of hand-holding and missionary position, and himself as the great emancipator of Lisa's clitoris. Then she added, "His idea of a special night when my parents were away was usually me pegging him in the basement while we watched fake lesbian porn on his iPad."

The frozen silence that followed was only broken when she said, politely but firmly, "If you ever tell anyone I just said that, I'll castrate you."

But Caleb never did. He never even felt tempted.

The shooting started between fourth and fifth periods, when the halls were packed with students. It was almost the end of the school year. The first bell sounded, and everyone spilled out of their classrooms. Some people went to their lockers to drop off or pick up books during the five minutes between bells. The air was hot and stagnant, the hallways rang with the smells of deodorant, perfume, and a hundred kinds of sweat; foods and soaps and lotions. All the things kids put on and inside their bodies, filling the halls as they jostled and slid past one another, intimate and anonymous at the same time.

PART TWO

The weird part was, Caleb had been thinking about breaking up with Lisa. She was going to Stanford, and he'd gotten into the University of Oregon. He didn't know how he was going to pay for school. He qualified for loans, but that made him nervous. Still, he figured he'd just move to Eugene, start school, get a job, and do his best to keep his debt down as he went. There was no question of not going. He'd been working a night job in the laundry room at a posh downtown hotel, and there was no fucking way he was going to spend the rest of his life doing stuff like that.

He liked Lisa a lot. But he'd been thinking about breaking up with her because they just didn't have much in common. They had fun together. But they were constantly running up against all the things that were different about them. That was tiring. And there was also just something about how sensible she was. Caleb had been with girls who told him they loved him after one or two times in the sack. Lisa never said it. Didn't seem to want him to say it. And she didn't talk about the future—about what they were going to do when college started. He assumed this was because she was planning on them breaking up. It just made sense, and she always did the thing that made sense.

She was very smart, and very pretty, and she was ferocious and hilarious and wonderful when they were alone. Sometimes she'd even surprise him with an off-color joke about oral sex, or she'd suggest they go see an action movie together. She could be a lot of fun. But it was a lot of work, and trying to do it long distance wouldn't make it any easier. Caleb had an idea about the arc of a person's life. Hard relationships could be good relationships—they could be the kinds of relationships that turned into something real. But they were for later; after college, certainly. High school was for fun relationships.

Plus, if he was being honest with himself, she didn't seem that into him. Not even as into him as he was into her. He didn't think she'd be too upset, really. He assumed she was thinking pretty much the same thing.

It seemed like such a given that he almost didn't think about it. Except that he did. Kind of all the time.

The shooting started on the first floor, at the north end of the school. Caleb was on the second floor, south end, because that was where his locker was. He didn't realize that he was hearing gunfire until the fourth or fifth shot, and then it was only because he also heard screaming. When Caleb turned around and looked down the long hallway that reached to the other end of the school, he could see a shock wave of reaction moving toward him, like an experiment in physics class. The students closest to the noises reacted first, and jostled into the students behind them—who jostled into the students behind *them*—creating a compression wave of fear and revulsion that rippled down the hall. Then the wave front began to collapse as panicked teenagers stumbled and fell in a tangle of arms and legs, scrambling, trampling one another.

Caleb was taller than most of the other students, so he saw what was headed his way. And he was standing next to an exit staircase, so he managed to get clear before the wave hit him. He ran down one floor and out of the building with a few dozen other early adopters who'd bolted before herd instinct took over and the stampede started. They all paused in the open field next to the school, and it felt like the whole world was inhaling to scream. Then more shots rang out, inside the building. Everyone else headed south, for the cover of the gym, a hundred yards away. But Caleb ran north, parallel with the wall of the building, toward the shooting. He stuck close to the bed of rhododendrons that grew next to the school as he went. The plants wouldn't stop bullets, he knew. But at least this way, if someone with a gun suddenly popped out of the doorway he was heading for, he'd have somewhere to hide.

Caleb had no idea what neurogenic bladder dysfunction was. He had to look it up on the Internet. Wikipedia described it as a condition common to people with spinal cord injuries, where the nerve pathways between the brain and the bladder are cut or damaged, so the bladder just empties or overflows or whatever. There were disposable catheters for people with temporary neurogenic dysfunction. If the condition was permanent, the doctors would basically put in a plastic bypass tube that would empty into a disposable pee bag. Forever.

PART THREE

Caleb thought he and Lisa made a weird couple. But if she agreed with him, she didn't let on. The differences between them, the ones that worried him so much, hardly seemed to make an impression on her. She actually seemed to find a lot of them funny.

A week before the shooting, Caleb took his little silver freestyle bike to pick Lisa up at her off-site internship. She was getting college credit for spending two days a week injecting radioactive tracking dyes into fish for the National Oceanic and Atmospheric Administration. Lisa was waiting for him outside the office in her casual business attire. She was sitting on a low concrete retaining wall on the waterfront, and as Caleb rode up she was handing something to a gutter punk girl about the same age as him and Lisa. The girl hustled off like she had something to hide, and Caleb coasted to a stop in front of Lisa.

"Hey, babe," he said.

"Hi, Caleb. No car today?"

"I'm saving the environment," he said with a grin. "Hey, did you give that girl money?"

"Yep."

"Lisa . . ."

"Caleb . . ." she mimicked.

"You shouldn't let everyone take advantage of you like that."

She arched an eyebrow at him.

"Yeah, okay," he said, acknowledging the pointlessness of giving her grief about her charitable impulses. "Where do you want to go for dinner?"

"You're supposed to have an idea for that, Caleb."

"Yeah, but—"

"Because, see, you asked me out to dinner, so you're supposed to know where we're eating. This is part of my new plan? In which you don't take me for granted? You may remember me mentioning this plan. I believe I brought it up during a lengthy discussion which I initiated last week for the specific purpose of explaining The Plan."

"I know, I know. Geez! I was just messing with you. I was thinking . . . Roscoe's?"

Roscoe's was an old-school burger stand down in Caleb's neighborhood that, for some weird reason, also sold the vegetarian burgers Lisa liked.

"Roscoe's would be lovely," she said. "How are we getting there?"

"Well, it's a nice night for a walk. Or, you know, I could ride you on my bike."

"What an excellent suggestion. I think it's a lovely night for a bike ride."

"Cool," he said.

She hopped down from the retaining wall and hitched up her khaki office work skirt. Then she straddled the back tire of his bike, put her hands lightly on his shoulders, and stepped onto the pipe-shaped pegs he had fitted to the ends of the axle on his rear wheel. With her hands on his shoulders, she could ride standing up on the back of his bike.

"You on there okay?" he asked.

She bounced experimentally on the pegs to test her footing. Her cool, dry hands were steady on his bare skin where his tank top exposed his shoulders.

"Ready to go," she said.

He stood up on the pedals and the bike rocked into motion, swaying back and forth as he leaned in to each push. She rode high behind him, flexing her knees to keep her center of gravity lined up with the rear wheel. All those dance lessons her parents got her when she was little, paying off at last, he thought.

She leaned down and spoke into his ear. "Can you keep this up all the way?"

"Shit," he said, and spat cleanly into the street. "You don't weigh hardly anything. I could keep this up all day."

She squeezed his shoulders and stood up straight again. He thought he heard her laugh.

W hen he came through the door closest to where he thought the shooting was, the first thing Caleb saw was Madison McCann lying in the stairwell, a few yards away. She was lying on her stomach with her head turned to the side, so he could see her face in profile. She looked surprised and scared, which made sense. She was also tangibly dead, which made no sense at all. There was a lot of blood. After staring at her for a second, Caleb realized that the side of her head that was resting on the floor was not all there, and that the stuff that he'd thought was clotted blood was actually small fragments of bloodstained brain matter.

A string of shots sounded up the hall to his right. He was still standing in the stairwell with Madison's body. He'd come in through an external set of double doors. Another set of double doors separated the stairs from the hall. The inside set was mostly closed, except that one of Madison's feet was caught between them. Which probably would have hurt, if she'd been alive.

Screw it, Caleb thought.

He stepped carefully around Madison, eased the door open, and took a quick peek up the hall. There was one kid walking slowly away, toward the south end of the building. Caleb recognized him immediately. Patrick Ressler. Another senior. With his broad, hunched back, olive drab Army jacket, and straight red hair, he looked like some kind of deadly parade float, ambling down the hallway, occasionally pausing to fire into a classroom. The hall was totally quiet now, except for the gunshots. When Patrick fired, Caleb could hear people trapped inside some of the rooms scream in surprise and fear. But Patrick didn't go into any of the rooms. He looked like he was headed somewhere specific, and shooting people along the way was just a sideline. Not worth stopping or changing course for.

Caleb stepped back and looked across the long north-south hallway Patrick was in, to the shorter east-west hallway at the end of the building. Patrick's locker was there. Caleb knew this because he'd seen Patrick there a bunch of times while he was chatting with Lisa, at her locker. Which was just across the hall from Patrick's locker.

The scene in the shorter hallway almost looked fake, because it seemed overdone. There were bodies, backpacks, and books all over the floor. There was blood spattered on the walls. The floor was almost completely covered with it. And Caleb could see he'd have to go out there, because he could see Lisa lying near her locker, and he could tell she was injured, and alive.

More shots, farther away.

Some of Caleb's mom's boyfriends had guns. Every once in a while one of them would take him to a range, but more often they'd just take him out to the woods and spend the day plinking cans and blowing up watermelons. So Caleb knew that shooting without ear protection of some kind, especially in a confined space, could really mess a person up: ears ringing, loss of equilibrium, eyes dazzled from the muzzle flash. Which meant that Patrick was either wearing earplugs, which seemed unlikely, or he was half-deaf by now. Either way, Caleb hoped Patrick wouldn't be too much aware of what was going on behind him.

Caleb would have to walk. If he ran, he'd slip and fall in the blood.

He glanced down the hall, to make sure Patrick's back was still to him—that he was still walking away. Then Caleb fixed his eyes on Lisa, and stepped through the doorway.

It took Caleb the better part of a week to visit her, even though her parents had been calling him for days by then. At first there was just too much going on. The cops locked everything down while they cleared the building, and the EMT's were doing triage. Then the cops started interviewing people while ambulances and helicopters took the survivors to hospitals. Caleb talked to a half dozen cops, then got taken to a hospital with about a hundred other kids who weren't actually hurt, but were covered in blood. Someone had decided it was better to be safe than sorry. So five hours after the shooting, ER nurses cut Caleb's clothes off him, checked him over for injuries, filled out a report that included a diagram of all the places he didn't have bullet holes in him, and sent him to the hospital cafeteria in blue hospital scrubs, with his wallet, pocket change, and keys in a plastic bag. His mom and aunt were waiting for him there, and that was a whole embarrassing scene with a lot of crying.

They drove him home. He walked into his room, dropped his bag of stuff on the floor next to the bed, kicked off his bloody shoes and socks, and slept for fourteen hours.

He found out later that Lisa was in surgery for most of that time.

When he woke up, his mom told him school was closed for the week, and the neighborhood was crawling with reporters. Someone from the school district office had come by and given them contact information for trauma counselors and grief counselors, paid for by the district. So many strangers were calling their apartment that they stopped answering the landline.

It was around the third day that Lisa's parents started calling Caleb and leaving messages on his cell phone, saying Lisa wanted to see him. But he spent that day in his room, with the lights off and a pillow over his head.

He got the messages on the fourth day, but he didn't go visit until the fifth day.

Caleb didn't pay attention to the other people in the hallway. Most of them seemed to be dead or unconscious, but that wasn't why he ignored them. He ignored them because something in his mind was whispering that if he paid attention to them, he'd have to stop and deal with them—or he'd have to live with the memory of making a choice not to. So he stayed focused on Lisa. He walked stiff-legged, clenching the muscles in his ass, thighs, and back, so he wouldn't slip in the fresh blood that covered the floor. He walked the twenty feet across the long hallway where Patrick Ressler was shooting people, and he didn't look to his right, toward where he'd last seen Patrick, because there was nothing he could do about it.

Lisa was lying on her back, near her locker. Her head was barely touching the wall, and she was breathing in quick, shallow gasps, while her hands twitched around her midsection like injured birds. Her navy blue skirt was hiked up around her waist. Her green tights were sopping with gore from the blood on the floor, and her white Keds had gone a splotchy dark cherry red. Caleb knelt down next to her, but he didn't look at her eyes. Not yet. He looked at her hands, and lifted the edge of her shirt so he could see the small hole, just under her belly button, that was pumping out thick gouts of blood.

Someone in the hallway was crying. Caleb wished they'd be quiet. He didn't want Patrick coming back.

He took his pocketknife out—the one he wasn't supposed to have at school, but carried anyway—and cut a piece of the hem off of Lisa's skirt. Then he rolled it up like a tampon, gauged the thickness, jammed one end of the roll of cloth into the hole in Lisa's stomach, put his hand over it, and, finally, looked at her. Her eyes were wandering in their sockets, but they settled on him and he saw the recognition there.

"This is going to hurt," he whispered.

One of her twitching hands landed on his wrist and stilled. They locked eyes, and she nodded just the tiniest bit.

Caleb leaned on the wound, putting pressure on it. Lisa inhaled deeply, and passed out. Or he hoped she passed out. He held still, keeping pressure on the wound.

He heard more shooting in the hallway behind him. He didn't turn around. Then the fire alarm came on and he jerked in surprise and nearly lost his hold on the wound. Still, he kept his hand on it and kept leaning down, and the shots were further apart now, but he felt like they were closer to him. It didn't matter. There was something wrong with the blood around Lisa's body. It wasn't just the blood that had been there when he'd started. There was more. She was still bleeding from somewhere. The shots were definitely getting closer now, but that was fine. Caleb reached under Lisa with his free hand and felt something weird on her lower back. It felt like someone had scooped out a big chunk of her back and filled the hole with raw hamburger.

Exit wound. The term popped into his head. Every so often someone in his neighborhood would get shot, so Caleb was familiar with the idea of an exit wound. Little hole where the bullet goes in, big hole where it goes out. He needed—

"Goddamn it," he muttered. And as quickly as he could, he stripped off his T-shirt, wadded it into a ball, lifted Lisa's side, and jammed the shirt into the hole in her back. Then he resettled her and leaned on the wound in her stomach, using his weight to press her back down on the wadded-up T-shirt.

The last three shots had been just around the corner. Patrick was close. It didn't matter. And suddenly the doors behind him crashed open—the ones he'd come through, where Madison Mc-Cann was dead. And someone yelled, "Freeze! Police! Put your hands where I can—"

Caleb closed his eyes. A long burst of sustained gunfire and it was over.

O n the fourth day after the shooting, Caleb tracked down the EMTs who'd taken Lisa to the hospital. The messages her family kept leaving said the bullet had damaged her spine. They

were rambling, exhausted messages, and they used terms like neurogenic bladder dysfunction. So Caleb tracked down the right
EMTs, and, when he got ahold of one of them, he explained how
he'd found Lisa, and how he'd almost missed the exit wound. How
he'd rolled her partway over to pack his shirt into the wound.

"You did right," the EMT said, cutting Caleb off before he was
halfway through his explanation. The EMT's name was Igor. He
had a Russian accent, and a calm, unflappable manner on the
phone.

"But is it possible . . . maybe I hurt her spine?" Caleb asked.

"Maybe you did. But probably not. Okay? And she would bleed
to death if you not plug exit wound. Dead. No question. So you
address problems in right order. And like I say—about the spine,
probably nothing to do with you."

"Is it what you would have done?" Caleb asked.

"Me? No. I have backboard. Coagulant powder to stop bleeding. Half-million-dollar ambulance full of equipment. But if I was
you, with T-shirt and pocketknife? Yeah. It is what I would have
done."

"Thank you," Caleb said.

"Is nothing. Listen. You did good, kid. Other things to worry
about now. Don't worry about this. Go see girl. You did right. Save
her life. Understand?"

So on the fifth day he went to see her. The room was crowded.
Her parents were there. And her younger brother and sister. The
family's pastor. Lisa's grandmother, a little gray bird of a woman in
a knitted shawl and a dress that seemed to be made of cobwebs.
And Caleb's mom, standing awkwardly in the doorway in her

frayed jeans and off-brand sweatshirt. Everyone was acting like it was a party. Lisa's dad kept shaking Caleb's hand, and her grandma kept pulling him down and kissing his cheek. And then Lisa looked up from her hospital bed and said, "Okay, guys? I'd like a moment with Caleb, please." But she had to say it three more times before they left. Caleb smiled and waved awkwardly as everyone filed out. Some of them winked. Some smiled. Only Caleb's mom looked in any way concerned.

When they were gone, Caleb and Lisa looked at each other and she gestured for him to come over to the bed. She reached for his hand, and there were a bunch of tubes in her arm, but he ignored those and took her hand. And it was weird. She looked so different, so tired and broken. But her hand felt the same. She felt the same to him, even if she wouldn't look him in the eyes.

"So listen," she said. "I . . . guess I'm a paraplegic now."

He nodded. "They said that. Over the phone."

"My bladder wasn't working right. That was pretty upsetting. But I guess some of the problems were just from swelling. I've been getting a little more feeling back, and that started . . . some things work better than others. But they're saying I might not walk again. And the bullet. Went through my—uterus. So that's done too. My bladder works again though. So yay. I guess."

"I'm sorry, Lisa."

"Me too. But listen." She paused and took a deep breath, and he was almost relieved to see she was crying. "When I was in the hall. Before you got there. I had some time to think. And one of the things I was thinking was, I should have told you how I felt when I had the chance."

Caleb raised his eyebrows.

"But I feel weird about it now," she said. "After what you did. I wouldn't want you to think I was just grateful. Still. I promised myself I'd tell you, so I love you. That's all. I didn't say it before because I guess I felt silly, going right from Phil to you. Like I didn't seem to be able to make it on my own. So I figured we'd go our separate ways to college and there was no point making a thing out of it, but I really—you've made me so happy. The whole time we've been together. That was what I wanted you to know, while I was lying there. What I wished I'd said."

Caleb looked down at her, and something went out of him. Like he'd been holding his breath for weeks, and he finally let it go.

"Hold on," he said as he let go of her hand. There was a big reclining chair in the corner, designed for family members to sleep in during overnight stays. He went around behind it and pushed it up next to Lisa's bed. Then he climbed into it and took her hand again.

"I'm just getting comfortable," he said. "I'll be here for a while, so I should be comfortable. Anyway, there was something I was thinking about too. While I was sitting there in the hall, wondering if Patrick was going to come back, there were things I was wishing I'd said to you. A bunch of things you should know."

He was avoiding looking at her, but he could feel her move. She seemed to sit up a little taller, and she squeezed his hand where they touched on the dry linen of the hospital bed. He thought he heard her laugh. She said, "Tell me now."

And he began.

COFFEE CHAMELEON
Jay Clark

I have no one to blame but myself for my addiction, thanks to her no longer responding to my texts. She's moved on. So to speak. We still attend the same high school. She's been seeing a biker there—the kind that willingly wears spandex, not leather. He probably has other characteristics? I bet he looks environmentally friendly while putting on his helmet at 3:39 p.m.

I'm early again. She usually kisses the facial defect above his chin strap three minutes from now. Thoughtful of me to continue giving her the opportunity to 1) sense my presence in the parking lot; 2) be excited about what that could mean this time; and 3) walk out to my car and begin the process of letting me take her back.

Not proud of myself; just miss her a lot. Little things, of course. Like how she always happened to have a banana in her purse when I was hungry. And how she'd laugh at my "Is that a banana in your purse, or . . . ?" line as if it were sucking less with age. And how she implemented mandatory kissing breaks from studying, giving me her grade-improvement guarantee. And how she repainted my room a variation of the same grayish-blue color three times because she wasn't sold on me liking it enough.

That last little thing was probably a warning sign.

As is the biker pedaling directly toward my lurking spot. I can take him, provided I remain in my car. He parks beside my window and knocks on the glass. Does that mean I have to open it? Cracking it instead.

"She's not coming back to school," he says. To me, presumably. I'm not looking him in the eye.

I remember the first time I took one of Andi's pills like it was exactly 221 days ago. We were in her room, and she kept glancing at her second-story window as if her mom were about to dangle down from the roof any minute (not sure why her mom would've cared, given that she put her daughter on the stuff back in middle school). Eventually, Andi caved . . . right before changing her mind again, saying guiltily, "I can't—you're already too motivated, Matty." I swallowed one behind her back so she wouldn't be racked with guilt. Then I took off my shirt and built her a custom shoe rack from scratch.

Meanwhile, the biker hasn't left yet.

"Sorry, who's not coming back?" I say, playing dumb.

"Andi, you dick."

I ask him what comedian Andy Dick has to do with anything, steering the conversation back toward nowhere.

I didn't expect *my* Andi to be happy about me getting my own "prescription." Yet I still had the nerve to hope for a laugh after my "only because you've gotten so good at hiding yours" explanation. She insisted on coming with me, trying to talk me out of it on our way to the gas station across from Walgreens, where I purchased pills from a Craigslist-advertising college student in his midforties. After I told her the pills made me feel like I could step out of my brother's shadow someday, she stopped threatening to throw them into the automatic car wash I was taking us through so no one could see us fighting. As the spaghetti-noodle sponges slapped against the windows, she let me put my hand on her leg again. Then we had the kind of celebration that only crackheads can have, me shaking the pills to the tune of "Here Comes Santa Claus" and coercing her to dance along. For a moment, she let herself love it . . . me. God, I loved her.

"She's finishing the rest of senior year at college, doing post-secondary," the biker says, and a traditional punch in the face would've been much less painful. He goes on to tell me they broke up—not because I deserve to know, but because he wants me to stop driving by his house and spooking his mom.

I make a doubtful noise to indicate he must be thinking of someone else, so he shows me a picture of my car on his cell phone, my license plate clearly illuminated by a neighborhood streetlight. It kind of looks like me hitting rock bottom, night after night. Dude has a lot of pictures.

"Please tell her I'm sorry."

"Tell her yourself," he says, biking away from my car before I can explain I meant his mom, not Andi. Or maybe he got it right.

Andi insisted we always take our Adderall together, for safety reasons. Which led to her asking impossible-to-answer-innocently questions, like, "Be honest, did you swallow a pill when you were in the bathroom just now?" We'd clink dosages and say "Cheers"

prior to beginning tasks we'd normally have little desire to complete—
e.g., making lists and misdiagnosing ourselves with chronic illnesses.
"I'm ninety-five percent sure I have Lyme disease," she'd say, and
I'd counter with some sort of selfishly rare cancer that only I could
get. Then I'd kiss the side effects from her lips, and for about thirty
minutes, it felt like we could conquer the world . . . or, if nothing
else, get really excited about the world (from behind our computers) before it started seeming like everyone at the coffee shop was
out to get us.

She realized we had to change while I was still in my "Why—
what's the problem?" stage. Tried to get me to quit with her so we
could have "a sane start to senior year." I shouldn't have made fun
of her sobriety tagline, nor should I have accused her of spending
a decent chunk of time thinking it up. Maybe then she would've
explained that she was sugarcoating an ultimatum.

I'm one of the last to leave the school parking lot. Tomorrow
I'm quitting everything that I've done today.

I feel like a different person when I wake up the next morning. A
shittier me who wants to kill the saintly fuck who sprinkled his
pills into the neighbor's pond last night, as if there were some sort
of ash-spreading nobility to the good-bye.

Wish I didn't have to make the mistake of getting up for school,
but I've been cursed with parents who care if I live up to my brother's
potential. They'll be proud when I graduate as valedictorian, just
like him, in a few months, but only because they don't know enough
about my recent behavior to be properly disappointed.

It takes me thirty tries to put my contacts in, so this is my brain off drugs, unfortunately. While in the kitchen microwaving a bowl of instant oatmeal, my body moves slowly enough to worry my mom. I refuse the let-me-smell-your-breathalyzer she tries giving me at the kitchen table, as is my right, but she does it anyway. I don't ask if I pass.

"You'd tell me if you were on drugs, right, Matty?"

I freeze for a second—*Do pharmaceutical drugs that weren't originally prescribed to me count?*—before shaking my head. "You're thinking of your other son."

I sit up straighter and give her a kiss on the cheek when she threatens to drive me to school in her bathrobe.

Good thing she doesn't see me getting into my car, which requires a series of maneuvers that wouldn't visually make sense given I don't have arthritis. *Maybe being in a classroom setting will motivate you as freakishly as it did before you conditioned your brain and central nervous system to crave chemical stimulants,* I tell myself. It makes me laugh and laugh, straight through a stop sign. I act less sober when I'm clean.

Later that evening, I'm really busy feeling like cold turkey ass, as well as convincing myself my supplier was lacing his stuff with low-quality cleaning products. I still want to text him my order, and would if I hadn't deleted his number last night in anticipation of my own weakness. My arm just fell asleep. I miss Andi.

I spend the rest of the week incorrectly reassuring myself that at least tomorrow is Saturday.

It's finally Saturday, probably. A lot of exciting things are happening exclusively on TV. Haven't moved; *have* eaten an entire bag of Starburst, minus the one that fell on the floor and was quickly eaten, wrapper and all, by my German shepherd. He wouldn't tell me if it was a pink one.

"You sure you're okay?" Dad asks from my bedroom doorway, several hours later, after my situation doesn't evolve.

I pinch the wrong two fingers together into an okay sign, and even the dog looks ready to sit down for an intervention. I ask Dad if he'll make me a can of cinnamon rolls, which is more a question for Mom to ponder while eavesdropping from the hallway. I can see the edge of her house slipper. Dad promises to eat only two, give or take. I smile to myself. Then give my past self a hard time for being so caught up in my problems that I forgot how much I don't hate being around my parents at all. My mom doesn't wait until they're downstairs to give Dad her opinion.

"He's finally letting his heart finish breaking . . . and it's breaking my heart."

"Mine too, honey."

"Is there anything we can do?"

I hear him patting his stomach and saying something about cinnamon rolls.

My parents deserve to look at something less pathetic in return for the problem-free childhood they've given me. So I get up. I creak down the stairs. I watch TV in the chair beside Dad's while Mom reads on the couch. And I wait for everyone to be really, really tired before I start telling the truth about my withdrawal symptoms.

Mom and Dad stare back at me after I'm finished kicking off my own intervention, their expressions a mix of concern, hopefully a little bit of love, and probably a lot of disappointed-sounding inner dialogue, like, *Wow, we didn't realize we raised you to make such poor decisions.*

"At least it's not meth," I feel the need to point out.

Mom quietly rejects my lesser-of-two-narcotics rationalization, and reminds me this is serious: "*Matty. You have an addiction.*" Then her face softens. "We're glad you told us, though. So we can get you help."

I slouch deeper into my chair, the repercussions of being honest starting to hit me.

"Yes, help," my dad repeats. "This isn't a problem to sit on and hope it resolves itself, Matthew."

"Is that any way to talk about my favorite stalling tactic?"

Dad calculates aloud what that throwaway joke just cost me—he's thinking an extra therapy session each week. Won't cost him a penny—not with his co-pay-proof medical insurance.

"Does all of this self-destructiveness . . . Is it because of what happened with Andi?" Mom can't help asking.

I look down at the rug underneath the coffee table, eyes scanning the maze-like pattern for a loophole out of answering. Anything I say in response will come off as either too vague or like a blame-shifting betrayal of Andi and our broken relationship.

"He doesn't have to get into that right now, honey," my dad says.

"He doesn't?" I ask this on behalf of Mom, who's in shock that I'm being let off her hook.

Dad shakes his head. "You'll need something to talk about with your therapist *thrice* a week."

Mom supposes that's only fair, for now.

ONE MONTH LATER

My therapist—a calm Asian psychoanalyst in his fifties who specializes in treating substance abusers like me—doesn't think my after-I-quit confession makes my addiction to Adderall any more acceptable, either. His opinion is both professionally understandable and annoying. Been trying hard not to get along with him, but he doesn't seem to care.

"What if . . . what I was really addicted to all along was Andi?" I ask him one day, as if my sarcastic epiphany is out of the blue. Every Monday, Wednesday, and Friday, I find an awkward opening to bring up Andi, and then refuse to talk about her. No idea why. I guess it kind of makes me feel like I'm regressing toward getting back together with her—a clear indication that I'm nowhere near ready for a breakthrough of that magnitude.

"Remind me who this Andi is again?" Dr. Consunji asks, in case I've forgotten about his impish, twinkly-eyed sense of humor.

"I haven't introduced you to my other personality?"

Ignoring me, he says, "Know what I think?" and points to the side of his blue argyle sweater vest like there's a thorn in it. "I think you're still afraid of what this feels like."

"Looks pretty painful," I say, and make a face like he might want to get it checked out.

Dr. Consunji and I are quite the repetitive pair. I do my fake-Andi-revelation bit, then he does his fake-thorn-in-side routine and smiles like he'll be happy to get real when I'm ready. Then it's time to go, maybe we'll get somewhere next time.

"See you in less than forty-eight hours," I say on my way out the door.

Dr. Consunji loves it when I run out of topics to avoid discussing—it counterintuitively makes his day. So one morning, knowing it's a trap but still hoping to burst his bubble, I just decide to talk about *it*. Whatever the hell he's pointing to—the bowel movement, the thorn, the fear.

"Maybe I have one or two future ulcers," I admit.

Several, it turns out. My fear of failure, fear of being the last one to know everything's changing (even as the people I love are warning me), fear of never getting a chance to show them I can change along with it. One by one, I address what's gnawing at my insides and we let the shitty possibility of it coming true sit there between us for a mind-numbing number of grandfather-clock ticks. Then he gives me the tweezer-shaped signal to pluck the thorn away and I make-believe as I'm told. And it feels just as hokey when we go through the same extraction process during our next session . . . but also better than nothing. Here's what I think I'm learning: You've gotta stay on top of your fears. Ride their asses before they crawl back up your ass and make you feel stupid for not being anal-retentive enough to ignore that they're in there sucking the life out of you.

"Is that what I'm supposed to be learning?" I ask Dr. Consunji.

He refuses to answer the question. "Because it's not yours." (It's my fear talking.)

Andi taught herself to stop living in fear—of what would happen if she quit taking Adderall, in particular—and that's why she was able to change, move forward. She loved me enough to try to drag me along with her, but I wasn't ready. I was scared. I realize that now . . . too belatedly, I fear. Better add that one to the list.

FOUR MONTHS LATER

Graduated valedictorian last weekend, after all. Andi smiled at me once during my speech, then disappeared before I could tell her congratulations. No Adderall relapses to date, but still in therapy thrice weekly and grounded until it's physically impossible for me not to be.

"We're working on ways to hold you accountable in college, too," Mom keeps promising, usually while jingling the keys to the car that I might drive again in my late twenties, if I'm lucky.

"I'm most excited about our unannounced visits to your dorm room," Dad keeps chiming in, to further emphasize my future embarrassment.

In their own very suburban way, they make a scary team.

Truth is, I'm probably not the "responsible young man" they think I should be before they trust me again. But I've stopped doing most of the stuff that was distracting me from dealing with my assorted anxieties and turning me into an unnecessarily ambitious ex-boyfriend monster with lame sibling rivalry issues. Haven't quit missing Andi yet—seeing her smile at me again refueled those flames for at least another century—but lately I'm not as afraid to address the sucky feeling of missing her . . . before plucking it out and trying something new that pales in comparison to her. Activities like making sales calls for Dad out of the kindness of my being punished, getting a haircut twice, and spacing out in the living room.

For today's new letdown, I've walked a mile to the nearest coffee shop. I'm sarcastically hoping there will be a long line extending back to the door for me to wait in, and sure enough, there is. "Is the coffee any good here?" I ask the barista when finally I reach the front. Her name tag reads *Vanessa*, and she stares at me from behind thick glasses with eyes that seem to be saying, *Your coffee jokes are weak, I'm only here for the summer, and there's nothing remotely attractive to see underneath these horn-rims!* Except that third one's a lie—there's no hiding from that kind of pretty. Suddenly, I'm nervous.

She grants me a smile. "It'll taste amazing under one condition."

"What's that?"

"*You* want it to taste amazing."

"I don't trust myself to draw those types of conclusions," I say, while making too much eye contact with the bowl of bananas on my right.

"Then I'd get the iced white mocha with whip." Vanessa doesn't tell me it's also known there as the "sorority girl special" until after I decide to order it. She puts a smiley face on my cup, though, as I look down at the plastic box that\ says *TIPS* and frown.

"Would you believe me if I promised to bring your tip tomorrow?"

She clicks her tongue twice and nods. "If I had a dollar for every time I believed that . . ."

"Right. You could buy a new . . . life-changing whatever-you'd-like."

"A nicer shampoo, maybe," she says with a dreamy twirl of her dark hair.

I want our conversation to continue a lot more than the twenty customers behind me do. I push through the door with mocha in hand, the bell jangling, wondering if she feels the same underneath those weird glasses.

I remember to give Valorie a dollar the next day. (She's changed the name on her tag, but the coffee shop is even busier, so I don't have time to ask why.)

I give Vanna the four quarters I found on my parents' dresser the day after that. She tells me she's almost saved enough for a haircare brand that's slightly better than Suave (and that she regrets being Vanna today, because *Wheel of Fortune* watchers can't get past the White). So the next day I bring her two dollars and recommend she dream bigger. Vivian says she'll split them with Vanna and relay the inspiration.

I start hanging around more and more, "but not anywhere close to closing time," per my mom's Crazy Matty instructions. Just an hour here and there, at the table in the corner, where I can still sneak looks at her making drinks. Sometimes she comes over and cleans the table next to mine (on days when Mom doesn't insist on joining me), a few strands from her choppy haircut falling into her face, while I pretend to be doing something really smart for a good cause on my laptop. I like the way she sweeps the area of the floor that I've already been cleaning up for her when she's not looking . . . takes her time when she moves . . . the curvy figure she still manages to cut even while trapped behind a mandatory apron.

It always takes much more courage to talk to her when she's out from behind the counter, though. One day, I say something uninteresting to her about how she's not wearing her glasses. I have to repeat myself before she stops sweeping and looks over.

"My sister hid them from me," she says.

"As a joke?"

"Out of spite."

"Don't you need them for . . . sight?"

"Yes. But that's not how her revenge system works." She dumps the contents of the dustpan into a nearby trash can, asking if my mom will be joining me today.

"She's probably hiding inside that trash can over there, with your glasses."

She laughs, and I offer her the seat across from me, in case she wants to pretend she doesn't work here for a few minutes. She declines, preferring to pretend she's working while secretly taking a break.

"I like your shirt, by the way," she says, squinting. "The color matches your eyes."

"Thank you." I sneak a glance down to make sure my polo is still red, and that's when she tells me she was kidding. She's about to walk away when I ask if she'd ever consider hanging out with me. "When you're not, uh, being paid to or whatever?"

She blows her hair away from her forehead, amused. "I've always wanted to go on a date with a customer who could make me sound like a prostitute unintentionally."

"Then I'm your guy," I mumble, before apologizing profusely.

What can I say, I have a way against words.

D on't ask me how, but a few days later, it's a date. She walks out to the car wearing a summery orange-and-white-striped halter dress, no apron, still no glasses, her choppy hair pinned back from her face. I'll have to assume she smells great until my cologne dies down. I wait as long as possible before letting her in on where we're going. She opens the window and doesn't jump out of it, instead saying she loves the zoo.

"I can't tell if you're being serious or not."

She smiles. "Does it really matter, White Mocha?"

"Not really, Vuuh . . . ?"

"Ronica."

"But now I owe my mom ten dollars, Veronica."

She thinks it's endearing that I'm the kind of guy who asks his mom for first-date ideas and then bets against them being well received. I tell her it was either that or my dad's "family movie night at our house!" suggestion. Then I say she looks really, really pretty during nonworking hours. We spend the last fifteen minutes of the drive playing Guess Which Wild Animal Noise I'm Making? I text my parents when we get there, thanking them for not coming with us.

On our way to the entrance, she asks a perfectly reasonable question that throws me backward into dangerous territory.

"Have you always been so—how do I say it—frequently in touch with your parents?"

"Kind of a long story," I say, after a lengthy pause that would've given me plenty of time to start it. I cover up the topic with an oddly timed cheetah growl. She guesses howler monkey, but then changes it to hippo.

As we walk toward the Africa exhibit, I take her hand into mine, explaining it's for her own safety and the animals might not have been fed yet. For the rest of the day, I insist on keeping her out of harm's way.

For our next date, she decides we should sleep together. On top of a blanket in the dog park.

"But we haven't even kissed yet."

"Maybe because we're so tired." She yawns, ready for her nap. She holds the blanket open for me to join her, and when I do, she gives me a peck on the cheek. Then the weirdest thing happens. We both attempt to sleep, during the day, in public, at the same time. I've never performed such non-acts with a girl as beautiful and calm as her before.

At one point, she says, "I have to figure out the cat box . . . it's missing."

"Someone brought their cat box to the dog park?" I ask, after realizing she's sleep talking.

"I'm going back to the aquarium," she answers, more to herself than me, and then she returns to her unconscious investigation. I like that I can hear her voice as I fade out.

She's awake when I wake, sleepy eyed, her head propped in her hand. Before I can start thinking, she kisses me. Hard. Like she's been wanting to try a white mocha for a while.

TWO MONTHS LATER

I can't remember how many dates we've been on, which is good. However, I have a bad feeling about ice-skating at the indoor sportsplex tonight. Her idea, after my mom whispered it into her ear during family movie night. As we step out onto the rink, I insist on holding her hand. "For romance purposes, not balance," I claim. Approximately twenty near concussions later, I'm ready to go pro and about to attempt my first ever triple toe loop. I end up two-footing and two-arming "the landing" before clinging to the ledge for support. "Singled it," I say to her in mock frustration. She laughs (supportively) before insisting on making an attempt herself. She looks as graceful as my mom's favorite skater, Dorothy Hamill, when she ends up biting it. She makes an ice angel to pass the time it takes me to wobble over and help her up.

An hour later, we're starving. But not enough to wait in line with the tweens at the snack shop. Without thinking, I ask if she has any candy hidden inside her puffy coat. "Or maybe your bag?" Jokingly, I reach into her front pocket and pull out a banana. *Is that a banana in your purse, or . . .* The spell we've been dating under starts to crack.

Do we have to let it? I always thought I'd want to go back there, to where we were and why this or that happened the way it did, and how we could prevent the same bad decisions from hurting us again. But now that I'm here, back with this present-day version of her, it's so much different. And all those things from the past are falling under one of those meaningless lists we used to compile, which no longer seem important enough to work our way through.

I'm still holding the banana. She's still waiting to see what I'll do with it.

"This doesn't look like yours," I say, examining the peel and narrowing my eyes suspiciously.

"Maybe it's someone else's," Andi says with a small, cautious smile. "If we want it to be."

I answer by taking her hand and leading her back toward the snack shop, saying, "Hopefully the line is even longer now." It is—I need to stop with the sarcastic predictions.

"Did you know that certain species of gummy bears contain ten percent of your daily need for vitamin C?" I say, like we're back at the zoo.

She shakes her head. "I learn something from you every day, White Mocha."

"Likewise, Veruca Salt."

"Oh, it's Veruca Pepper now."

And that's how it should be—anything that keeps us from getting too comfortable, too set in our ways before those ways change into habits that we're deathly afraid of altering. In fact, she makes me feel like we'll never be too old to change our spots.

I smile and make an awkward leopard noise while leaning forward to kiss her.

HUSH
Marcella Pixley

If you have ever been shut inside, you know that you can smell the outdoors on someone. Mother always tells me this is how it was when I was a newborn. It was winter and I was a month premature. So tiny, the doctor told her to keep me indoors as long as possible, away from other people's germs and the snow that lashed at our windows. The way she tells it, I cried for the first six months of my life. She would lay me right down in her cello case and play Bach suites to keep me from colic and temper, my tiny hands clenched into red, shaking fists. More often than not, I imagine, I sang her accompaniment, opening the black square of my throat and screeching endlessly in my fury. Where is that fury now?

She says that when Father came home from the jazz clubs and let himself into the house, she could smell the outdoors on him, the sudden fresh smell of winter, how it lingered in the lapels of his tweed jacket, and when she buried her head in his chest, weeping, exhausted from her day with me, she would take in the scent of the outside world and it would be the only clean breath she got each day. Just the mint off my father's jacket. An instant. Alarming and fragile. It would last for as long as one inhale and then disappear, immediately overwhelmed by the perfume of diapers, dishes, and stale milk.

I leave my sandals on the porch steps and quietly close the door behind me so Mother won't hear it shut or feel the breeze, reminding her that I have been roaming about. I stand in the parlor, letting the outside lift from my skin and dissolve into the familiar closed-in scent of ninety-degree days and white starched sheets.

Mother is in our bedroom playing the Prelude to Bach's First Suite in G Major. I rub my face on the velvet armchair so I will smell like our familiar air and then climb the stairs, past all the closed rooms with their dusty memories and bad germs to our bedroom, which is the only place in the world where Mother feels clean.

She is beautiful when she plays. Her hair is unfastened and loose around her shoulders, only the first hints of gray starting to show through the brown, her arms relaxed, her spine straight. Mother always says that the cello is the only instrument that is built for perfect posture. The musician becomes a tripod with the instrument, two knees at right angles, feet planted on the floor, back strong and straight. Playing cello is the only time when Mother ever looks like part of the world.

I love to watch her play. To pretend this is who she is all the time.

I climb into our bed and lie on my stomach with my chin in my hands.

One time she told me the Prelude to Bach's First Suite is the most beautiful piece of music ever written for the cello, or for any instrument for that matter. It is a piece filled with echoes and reflections, one voice, singing lullabies to itself. It glides over strings, moving from resonant low notes to middle to high, breathing out like a fever breath on your cheek.

But there is irony in the Prelude. The piece, despite its apparent symmetry, does not actually stay the same. It does not rest in one octave, or repeat itself. Rather, the Prelude climbs almost invisibly, so you don't realize you've been moved until you look down and see that the world is falling away beneath you, swaying, at the limits of your vision, and you have no choice but to breathe and thank the Lord that you are alive. Because no earth that has mothers and cellos and Bach preludes in it can be all that bad, no matter how desperate it seems sometimes. There must be some germ of goodness.

I move back to lie on the pillows and listen to the last note of the piece ring out.

Mother raises her bow, a flourish. She lets the last note shimmer in the air before it begins to fade. Mother always tells me this is how you know an audience understands music. An ignorant audience breaks into applause as soon as the piece ends. They rise to their feet, cupping their hands, howling, "Brava! Brava!" trying to sound Italian. But an educated audience, like the audience that heard her play the Brahms sonata when she was a soloist at Herald Hall, the night they recorded her for the Vanguard record, her very last performance, now *that* audience knew how to wait until the last note died out—until the hall was almost but not quite silent—before filling it again with their thunderous applause.

Does Mother imagine applause as I lie in our bed tonight, my chin cupped in my hands? Does she imagine she is on that same stage, looking past the footlights into an audience that hangs on every note she plays? Or does she see the room for what it is—an antiseptic chamber that will hold her indoors like a pig in a form-aldehyde jar, keep her looking out of windows, wandering past un-used rooms, scrubbing her hands with bleach until they feel like hooves?

Mother looks at me with a strained smile. She sighs, puts her cello down, loosens her bow, and walks the music stand over to the side of our room with her bare feet.

She climbs into bed, moving behind me.

I feel her arms wrap around my belly. I let her curl into me. My mother's body. When I was a little girl I used to move closer to fit into her, but now when she does it, I hold my breath and stiffen. I'm glad she feels I am clean enough to love, today.

M other and Daddy rarely slept in the same room together, even before he got sick. Most nights Daddy would come home late, after the jazz clubs closed. He would put his music case by the door, pour himself a glass of wine, and fall asleep at the kitchen table, where we would often find him in the morning, with his tweed fedora tipped over his eyes.

He was a beautiful man. Tall. Soft-spoken. His eyes were deep and gray and he had the longest eyelashes, so that whenever I looked at his face I was compelled, even as a very small child, to take his hands and stroke them. When I was young enough to fit in his lap, I would cuddle up and scratch my fingers into his beard and kiss him until my lips tickled. Of course, this was before the virus sucked in his cheeks, spat out his beard, and left him a skeletal shadow of a man. I remember how he looked lying in the hospital bed they set up in the dining room so he wouldn't have to climb the stairs.

The dining room was the first place to fill with morning light and it had a high ceiling, so he wouldn't feel quite so closed in. Mother hired men to carry out the dining room table and move in the grand piano so he could spend the day playing music and listening to the radio. When he was tired, he could lie down. When he needed a bathroom, he could stagger across the hall. It's a wonder she was able to nurse him through the long year between his diagnosis and death. There was so much for her to clean up. Especially at the end. So much coming out of him. Arpeggios and cadenzas of sickness arcing from his body like final chords.

When things had finally progressed to the point where she knew the end was coming, when the doctor told her he's dying, and she knew that these words meant *now*, not someday, but *right now* in front of her face, she began closing off the rooms of our house. She told me it was because it was easier this way, to keep things clean. Daddy was allowed to be sick in the dining room and bathroom. I was allowed to play in the kitchen and my parents' bedroom. The other rooms, the places we used to pass through and touch—his study, Mother's music room, my old bedroom, the living room—were all off-limits now because it was too hard to know where exactly the virus was hiding.

That's when Mother first brought me into her bed at night, to make sure I was sleeping in a clean place, breathing good air and staying where she could keep an eye on me. I was eight years old.

Too old to share a bed with your mother, but too young to rebel against it, or to understand the disgust I feel now. Eventually, she moved me in full-time, and began calling it "our room" and meaning that it belonged to her and me, rather than her and Daddy.

In those early days, people didn't know much about AIDS. We didn't know if it could be left on doorknobs or toilet seats. We didn't know if you could get it if an infected person coughed or breathed on you. We didn't know if it traveled through tears, or if you could catch it through a kiss. And so when Daddy started dying, the dining room and the downstairs bathroom, his death rooms, were also off-limits to me. So I would sit in the hallway or at the kitchen table and call out to him *Daddy, Daddy,* and if he was awake he would call back to me *June Bug, June Bug,* which is how I knew he was still okay. No matter how bad it got, to me the man dying in our dining room was still just Daddy.

Even in the last weeks of his life, Daddy's music filled our house. It was played with weak and shaking hands amid jags of coughing and wheezing, but it was music nonetheless. He played the same jazz standards he had always played. To this day, anything by Gershwin will always bring me to tears. Sometimes, Mother would bring her cello into the dining room and jam along with him, making her instrument wail like the voice of Ella Fitzgerald, scatting around his melody, the sweet, chocolate riffs of a soul in mourning.

She was always tender with him. You hear stories about people who were abandoned by their loved ones when things got bad. Too much risk. Too many unknowns. Too much to clean up. Too depressing to watch the gorgeous young bodies, scourged and ravaged by a disease that seemed like a punishment for the sins and excesses of the previous decade. Free love in the seventies gave birth to full-body condoms in the eighties. And as a result, if it weren't for my mother's belief in *for better or for worse,* Daddy might have been part of a generation of elite young men who lived the high life when they were healthy—surrounded by the intellectual banter of novelists and musicians—but who, when things got messy, found the crowd parting for them to die by themselves in antiseptic hospital rooms, a staggering percentage of them developing full-blown dementia, as Daddy did in his final days, so that instead of spending their last moments saying good-bye to their loved ones and preparing to meet their makers, they raged in their hospital rooms alone, conversing with demons and angels who laughed at them with mouths filled with worms.

Even though she kept me from touching him, and even though she always made sure to scrub her hands with bleach and hot water whenever she had to deal with his accidents, Mother never left Daddy alone for too long. She would move between him and me, the strange dance of the caregiver, reading me poetry in the kitchen with a glass of milk and a grilled cheese sandwich, and when he called out, pulling on a pair of disposable latex gloves to hold his hand or rub his skeletal shoulders while he wept. Our trash bins filled with latex gloves, translucent and dry as snakeskins. I know she must have been terrified and overwhelmed. She loved him and she loved me. She wanted to help him die but she also wanted to keep me safe. Her job was to clean up what came out of his body and to comfort him in his pain, but also to give me kisses and braid my hair and put on my pajamas at night.

She had all kinds of ways to keep me occupied. Sketchbooks.

Modeling clay. Watercolors. When she went to him for too long, I would call for her, making sure my voice was loud enough for both of them to hear me in the other room. There was always something I needed. A glass I couldn't reach. A chair I couldn't lift. I was only eight years old. How was I to know that what I really needed was my mother and father in the same room with me again.

"Mommy!" I called out on the last day of his life, my voice shrill and strident so it would set her teeth on edge, make her jump to attention. "Mommy, I'm thirsty!"

Her tired voice came from the dining room. "Just a minute, June. Daddy needs me."

"I can't!" I called back. "I can't reach the glass!"

"Oh for goodness' sake, June Bug. Just climb up on a chair or something."

I punished her when she returned, shrugging my shoulders and making my body rigid when she reached toward me. When she offered me the glass of water I pushed it away and it fell to the floor. There was water everywhere but the glass didn't break. I remember being disappointed, because a broken glass would have been much more dramatic.

"Honey," she said. "Please try to understand. I'm doing the best I can."

"No, you're not," I said. "I told you I was thirsty and you didn't care."

"I did care," Mother said wearily. She knelt on the floor with a rag and started cleaning up the spill. "I do care, sweetheart. But Daddy needed me just then. Can you try to understand that? He needed me more than you did."

"Daddy always needs you!" I screamed in her face. "I'm tired of him needing you so much."

"God help me, June. Your father is dying. Don't you understand that?"

How could I have really understood?

"Why doesn't he hurry up and do it then!" I screeched. Then I turned my head toward the dining room and screeched, "Why don't you hurry up and die, Daddy. Hurry up and die right this second for all I care."

She slapped me. Suddenly. Furious and exhausted. I sank to the floor, stunned by my own tantrum and astonished at the force of her reproach. Then Mother knelt on the floor beside me. She was holding herself and sobbing.

"I'm sorry, Mommy," I whispered, crawling over to her.

She leaned her head against the wall and sobbed so hard, her breath was coming in shaking gasps. She did not look like my mommy. Where was my mommy who liked to take care of me, and who was this woman who looked so broken and so old?

"I didn't mean what I said, Mommy. I don't want Daddy to die."

She lifted her head to look at me. Her eyes were red and filled with shadows.

"I know that, honey," she said. "We're all so tired and so scared, we don't know what we're saying or doing anymore. You didn't mean to hurt Mommy."

I snuggled into her and put my head in her hair. "I did mean to hurt you," I said. "But I'm sorry. I was being mean. You forgive me, right?"

Mother kissed me on the forehead.

"Can I tell Daddy I'm sorry?"

"You can't go in his room, sweetheart, you know that."

"I'll stand in the hall. I'll tell him from there."

"Okay," Mother said. "I think that would be a good idea."

She took me by the hand and we walked from the kitchen into the hallway. It was not a long walk, just a few steps past the old dictionary stand and the bookshelves that reached to the ceiling, past the staircase and the window seat and the curving banisters leading up. It was not a long walk, but I remember how long it seemed, walking side by side from the kitchen to the dining room, holding Mother's hand and rehearsing the words I would say to him that would make him forgive me.

Daddy was lying in his hospital bed, facing us. His eyes were open.

"I'm sorry, Daddy," I said like a good girl. "I didn't mean the bad thing I said."

But it was too late. He was gone.

O utside our window, the last rays of late afternoon sun struggle past the window shades and slant into the room. They cast long dusty shafts under the drawn curtains, a swirling promise that there is such a thing as sky. Freedom and air and sunlight are still out there, even when I cannot see them. I lie next to her and I realize, with a small stirring of satisfaction, that even though she may be trapped in this dark house, I am not. Not really. I am June Bug Jordan. I am fourteen years old, for better or for worse. I can wander in the afternoons. If I'm quiet, I can pull up carrots

from neighbors' gardens and eat. I can steal string beans and to-
matoes. Summer is a good time for finding food. There is so much
of it growing in the neighbors' backyards, so much for the taking.
But I haven't had anything besides stolen vegetables today and my
stomach growls and protests.

"Mother," I say.

She kisses the back of my head and nuzzles my neck. Her breath
is too warm and her body is too close. It makes me feel dizzy. I
don't like the way she smells. I don't like the way the warm sheets
feel under my legs. I want to run out of there. I want to leap from
the sheets and fly. But something keeps me there, tethered to her.
What is it? Obedience? Nostalgia? Pity?

My stomach growls. We both hear it.

"Mother," I say. There is an edge in my voice. The slightest
knife's edge. "It's getting late. Is there anything to eat for supper?"

Mother lifts her face toward me. I can see the planes and ridges
of her jaw and her chin. How long has it been since I have seen
this woman put food into her mouth? A week? Could it have been
a whole week? How long can a person survive without eating?

"I don't think there's much food down there," she says. "But the
delivery man comes with groceries on Saturday again. I made him
a list. Guess what's on it?" Mother pulls herself up so she is sitting
cross-legged on the bed and smiling at me. It is a wild, glassy-eyed
smile. "Guess the foods, June Bug. Guess the foods."

"I don't want to guess," I say.

She never orders enough, and we always run out too soon.

"Then I'll tell you." Mother claps her hands. She is delighted
with herself. "All the things you loved when you were a little girl.

What did you love? Tell me. Tell me all the foods you used to love and I will tell you if I thought of them already for you."

I sigh. "Popsicles?"

"Yes sirree."

"And strawberries?"

"Of course strawberries. Lots of strawberries. Mountains of strawberries."

I feel myself smiling, suddenly. When I speak next, it is not with the voice of a fourteen-year-old girl, but someone much younger. An eight-year-old girl whose father is dying of AIDS, a very little girl, hungry and desperate. "And cheddar cheese and oranges and hot dogs and yogurt?"

"Yes, yes, yes." Mother laughs. She touches my nose with one finger. "And cold cuts, and yellow apples, and pickles, and rye bread, and salami, and all sorts of yummy things for you to make so you can eat and eat all you want."

"Like grilled cheese?"

"Of course," says Mother. "You know how to make grilled cheese. It's easy."

"But I'm hungry now, Mommy."

Mother frowns. "Oh, sweetie pie," she says.

"Can we go and look? Please? All I had today was a carrot."

Poor pathetic little girl.

Mother hesitates, a pause that is too long and too quiet. Then she makes herself smile. "We can go down and look," she says finally. "I think there might be one can of soup still. Chicken noodle, maybe. I can walk down the stairs with you. But you know I don't like going into the kitchen, June. The kitchen is so close to

the dining room. Anything could be coming through those cracks."
Her voice is broken.

"There's nothing coming through the cracks," I tell her.

"How can you be sure?"

"Please, Mother," I say softly. "Nothing is going to come
through the cracks. Nothing ever comes through the cracks."

She follows me reluctantly down the stairs. Then, as she always
does, she stops at the entrance to the kitchen, frozen in place. I
leave her clutching the banister, halfway into the kitchen, halfway
out. A ghost, lingering on the threshold. Then I make my way to
the empty cupboard on my own, as I always do.

She is right. There is one can of soup left. I find the old can
opener and a dented saucepan under the sink. There is an antique
stove, which I light with a match, a sudden scratch of sulfur and
smoke. The lit gas makes a blue halo around one burner. I stir
the soup with the wooden spoon and even though I know girls my
age are not supposed to make believe anymore, I pretend that I
am the mommy cooking good meals for her baby, and I want to
feed her and feed her so her belly will be full and she can grow.

See, little baby? Mommy loves you.

I stir and hum the kind of song I think a cooking mommy would
make.

Soon, the heat from the antique stove and the heat from the
summer day and the heat from the steaming soup fills the kitchen.
It glazes the windowpanes.

The steam rises and swirls like ghosts.

I pour soup from the saucepan into a bowl and then carry the
bowl to the empty table, still pretending to be the mommy, and

now I am both of them at the same time, so happy to sit and eat together. *Mealtime. Mealtime. Come and get it.* I sit down in the chair. I dip a spoon into the soup and feed myself a tiny sip. *Here you go, baby. Good for you. Yummy soup.* But then when I taste it, I suddenly realize I can't get it to go down fast enough with my spoon, even when I sip and sip one spoonful after another. I spoon soup so fast into baby's hungry, open mouth, she slurps and burbles. *So hungry, Mommy. So hungry I can't get full.*

I put the spoon down and pick up the bowl. Miracle of miracles. There are noodles and carrot squares and tiny wonderful cubes of chicken. I raise the steaming bowl to my lips and drink and drink until soup rolls down my chin.

"You are dripping soup all over the place," Mother mutters from the banister. "You're making drops on the table and on the floor. I knew this would happen."

"It's not a big deal, Mother," I tell her. "I'll just clean it and it will be good as new."

"It is a big deal," says Mother. "I saw the spatters. I know it's not good as new. It's soiled, June Bug. Can't you see that? I'm trying so hard to keep you from harm. You don't know who picked those carrots. You don't know who touched the chickens. You don't know what kinds of diseases they might have had in their skin."

"Mother," I say. My voice is cold, steely. "This is ridiculous."

"Are you calling me ridiculous?"

"No," I say. "I'm calling your worries ridiculous. Everything here is safe. Everything here is clean. Please. Let's just go back upstairs. I'll read to you until you fall asleep."

"How do you expect me to fall asleep? No, June. I am your mother. I am your mother. We need to disinfect this house."

"Jesus Christ," I say.

"Don't swear," says Mother. "It makes your mouth dirty. Your mouth is dirty, and it's doing dirty things, June."

"My mouth is fine," I say.

"It's disgusting. Help me disinfect. Help me do it right now. Are you going to help me? Are you going to help me clean up this mess, June? Are you going to help me make the house safe for you? All I'm trying to do is keep you safe."

"I don't want you to keep me safe."

Mother gasps. She looks like she has been slapped, and I think she is going to cry.

After the funeral, she held me and held me. We promised each other we would never ever let go. I leaned my head into her and curled my body into her and I breathed. I want to run to the door, swing it open, let all the air and sun and smells inside. I want to run out the door and down the street into the neighborhood where people turn their heads and I want to scream until I shake the sky.

Mother's hands are shaking. She is so thin. Thinner than Daddy was when he died. I can see her bones under her shirt, the two neck bones arcing like swans. I can see the pulse in her neck. Exit rebellion. Enter pity. Enter obedience.

"Okay," I say finally. "Okay, I'll help you."

"Oh, God bless you."

And so we begin. We return deliberately to our strange status quo.

All disinfections are methodical and specific in their order, each step designed to catch the germs left over from the last. There are rules that make sense. You always start from the highest places and work your way down. Germs from the ceiling can drip down on the walls. Germs from the walls can fall to the counters, can fall to the floor, can get trapped beneath your feet and then spread back into the rest of the house, so you always do the floor last with a brand-new bucket of bleach. It's important to protect your hands if at all possible, because hands invariably touch eyes and mouth and all the other inside places and then the germs attack the body.

There are also rules that are less obvious. Rules that will make your mind reel if you think about them long enough. For instance: Mother keeps crates of surgical gloves in the pantry and goes through an entire box during a typical after-dinner disinfection. According to Mother, you can only safely use a pair of surgical gloves for the disinfection of a single large item or three smaller items. Here are some examples of large items: a wall, a table, a countertop. Here are some examples of small items: a toaster, a faucet, a telephone. This rule invariably means that Mother needs to change gloves ten or fifteen times.

The main problem with the surgical gloves is that in order to take them off your hands, you have to use your fingers, which means touching the disgustingness.

Surgeons, of course, know how to do this without touching anything contaminated. First they rinse their gloves in antiseptic—in our case, Clorox bleach—then they remove one glove halfway, and the other halfway, and then they take the fingertips of one glove to put the other glove in the garbage and then use their bare fingers to remove the remaining glove, being careful of course to only touch the inside-out part, so as not to contaminate the skin.

The problem with Mother's method is this: she never trusts the inside-out part. What if there are trace elements of disgustingness under the glove? What if it somehow seeps through the microscopic fissures of the latex, or somehow, God forbid, under the fingernail, where it can fester and spread, nibbling at the cuticles and eventually destroying the entire finger, gnawing at the hand until it looks like hamburger? This terrifying dilemma means that she will sometimes get stuck in a never-ending loop of putting on and taking off surgical gloves until she is satisfied that she has performed the process with absolute and perfect precision.

The latex gloves make my hands dry. When she isn't looking, I peel the gloves off my hands and surreptitiously throw them away in the garbage. I work without them, trying my best to keep my hands out of her sight. She scrubs the counter with a bristle brush, back and forth, back and forth, back and forth, so hard that she grunts and pants with the effort, her breath coming out in jagged gasps. Her hands and her head are shaking, and she is making small whimpering sounds.

"Are you okay? You look like you're not feeling so good."

"I'm not," she says. "I'm feeling horrible."

Her voice is low. It is the sound of a person holding herself still because she does not want to fall through the ice. "You didn't wear gloves," she says.

"It's okay," I say. "I just took them off in the end."

"The end is when it matters most," she says. "Now you have disgustingness all over your body. All over your body, June."

"Not all over," I tell her. "It's just my hands. I'll just rinse them in bleach and then we'll be good as new, okay?" I grab a bottle of Clorox, walk quickly to the sink, and pour bleach over my hands.

I scrub and scrub. The bleach is cool at first, but after a while it burns. I stop scrubbing and show her my hands, the fronts and the backs. I show her how clean I am.

"It didn't work," says Mother. "You'll have to wash all of you. You need to take a bath with it."

"No one bathes in bleach."

"You have to, June. If you don't I can't get near you, sweetheart. You understand that, don't you? We can't get to sleep if you aren't clean. Please, June."

She is so thin and so desperate.

"Okay," I whisper. "Okay." But inside me something is screaming.

Mother gives me a weak smile. She takes another pair of surgical gloves out of the box. Then she reaches under the kitchen sink and brings out a brand-new white plastic bottle of Clorox bleach and a brand-new scrub brush.

I follow Mother upstairs. The door is ajar. I can see the claw-foot tub waiting to swallow me. Its toothless mouth is wide open.

Mother turns on the hot water. There is the sudden rush of current. Heat fills the tiny room with steam until my lips and my face are glazed.

Mother pours in the three caps of Clorox. The water begins to swirl and bubble and the scent of bleach rises into the room, a new kind of steam, sharp and toxic, the smell of hospital floors and swimming pools.

I put my clothes into a plastic trash bag, and Mother pushes the bundle out of the bathroom door with her feet.

Now the bath is ready. So hot, the room swirls in steam. I put one foot in, wincing at the scalding water. "It's too hot, Mother."

"I know," she says gravely. "It has to be."

I put the other foot in. Then I lower myself down, grimacing as the water closes over my legs. At first the heat is overwhelming, and I have to fight to keep myself inside. Every ounce of my body, every fiber wants to spring out of the water and run. But Mother has backed her crimped body to the door and she is standing there, bracing herself against the doorway, with tears coming down because she knows it hurts me, but she is going to see the process through to the end—to the very end when she will be able to touch me again because she knows I will no longer be disgusting.

When it is over, Mother helps me stagger from the bathtub and into a clean white nightgown. Then, gently, gently, she leads me to our room. She helps me into our white bed. I curl onto my side and pull the crisp sheets up to my chin, wrapping myself in the scent of bleach. Clean. Clean. All at once, I am too tired to keep my eyes open. My body is raw. My spirit is raw. The sheet against my elbows and knees feels like fire. I close my eyes and try not to cry.

Mother takes her cello out of the case, tightens the bow, pulls out the endpin, and sits on the stool by the bed. She plays the Allemande with such tenderness, remembering it nearly breaks me open.

Each note runs its fingers across my skin, each bow a smooth, cool palm. My eyes are closed in pain, so I can't say for certain if she is weeping, but it sounds like the piece is weeping, the lines rising and falling in a whisper and even though the key signature is G major, usually bright and optimistic in its timbre, tonight it is mournful, brooding, and deeply apologetic. *I would feed you if I could*, says the cello in the lengthening shadows of our bedroom. *I would touch you and hold you. I would open the windows and let the outside air come in. But I am made of wood. I am as trapped as you are. My foot is rooted in the ground and I am unable to make a sound. I have no voice except for when she plays.*

It is not medicine. It is an apology. The Allemande ends with a G major chord, two beautiful notes on the bottom and two on the top, the last one ringing into the room like a promise. When Mother finishes the piece, she closes the cello and bow back in the case and comes to lie down behind me. She pulls me close to her body, wraps her arms around me, and breathes into my neck until she falls asleep. I lie in front of her, curled against her grief, the air from her mouth and nose warming my skin like a fever that won't go away.

I lie awake for hours. I stare at the ceiling, using my mind to trace the crack in the plaster that splinters across the ceiling. I imagine different things that can snake. A fault line. A river of ink. A highway viewed from a hot air balloon. A track of ants. A long, narrow scar. I raise one hand from the blankets, close one eye, and use my pointer finger to trace the line across the ceiling. I am one tiny ant in a long caravan of ants, heading out of our sweltering room and into the distance. I am a car on the highway inching off into nowhere.

She mumbles something in her sleep and shifts position. I lift her arm from my waist and wriggle sideways like a salamander emerging from the mud, slowly, slowly, wincing as the bed brushes against my skin, squirming from the blankets and wriggling onto the floor, hands first, then belly, then legs—so that soon, I am on all fours on the floor, crouching in the dark, Mother's dream breath hissing into the room like thread drawn through cloth.

If I am careful, she won't hear me. If I am careful, she will never know I'm gone. It feels heavenly to be free of her. My body needs air. It needs space, the feeling of wind on my skin.

I crawl into the hallway where all the closed doors look at me like sideways, one-eyed faces humming lullabies through closed lips. I creep to each door and, one by one, touch each doorknob. When that isn't enough, I lick them, running my tongue across the smooth black roundnesses, trying to taste the vestiges of who we were when we were alive. Fingerprints have a flavor. Salt and sweat. Blood and dirt. I can almost taste them underneath the bleach. Glorious.

I am starving for more. I tiptoe down the stairs. Here is the heavy wooden door of the dining room where Daddy slept and lived and died. "I'm back," I whisper into the keyhole. I breathe in slowly, drawing the air from that hidden space into my mouth, tiny vestiges of his cells, his hair, his fingerprints swirling through the keyhole and into me. It fills me with something new, something that makes me believe that maybe, just maybe, I can do this. I open the dining room door. All at once, I am drowning in the scent of my father in his final days. The stripped hospital bed. The old photographs covered in dust. The grand piano, smiling at me with white-and-black teeth.

Here is the alabaster chandelier. Here is his tweed jacket and his old hat still hanging on their hook by the bed. I wrap myself in the tweed jacket and I coronate myself with the hat. The vestments of a dead man. I slide my body against the high walls of the dining room, stretching my arms like wings. I roll on his stripped hospital bed, petting the mattress, rubbing my face into the cloth. Then I twirl to the grand piano and slide my fingers over the tops of the keys without making a sound, gentle, gentle, just the lightest feather touch. I bring the sheet music up to my face and I inhale deeply, imagining the notes rising from the page and into my mouth, diving into my delirious lungs and into my bloodstream until I am utterly and gloriously infected. Can you see me? Can you see how full of music I am? If you cut me, jazz will shine from my skin, like Daddy at the piano playing Gershwin, his long, thin fingers flying across the keys like rain.

Upstairs, Mother curls into her own darkness. She breathes the same stale air she has been breathing for too many years. But I am not the same. I am not the same obedient ghost I was a few hours ago. My heart is beating. I open each window in the dining room. The outdoors seeps into the room like wind, licking its dark tongue across the windowsills and the walls, letting the outdoor sounds of things I had forgotten back into this house. The rush of a car going by. The staccato notes of a dog barking. The white sound of rain.

I push my face against the screen to feel the raindrops, but it is not enough. I need to raise my face to the sky and close my eyes and feel the cool petals of rain on my cheeks.

I spin to the piano and play one glorious minor chord.

D minor. Sad. Broken. But hopeful.

"June?" It is my mother's voice.

I hug Daddy's tweed jacket close around my shoulders and

slowly, slowly back away from the piano, away from the stripped hospital bed and away from the dining room. I leave the door and the windows open.

"June," calls Mother again, muffled in blankets.

Her voice is so weak.

I turn from the dining room and hurry down the hall, past the heavy Victorian dictionary stand, past the bookshelves, past the closed rooms on either side, and down to the heavy oak door in the front hallway.

"June?" It is my mother's voice again.

I turn the brass doorknob with both hands and pull hard. I put muscle into it. And then the door is open, and I am standing in the dark, wet square of night. I step onto the porch where the rain is slanting sideways. I do not close the door behind me. I want the rain to come in. I walk down the porch stairs, past the gray pillars. Cool rain glazes my cheeks. I stand on the wet gray flagstones. I turn and raise my face.

I look at my house from the outside.

How long has it been since Mother has seen our house from this angle, from the neighborhood side, from the side of people who are living and breathing? Anyone walking down Trowbridge Road at night can see what I am looking at right now: the ivy snaking along the clapboard, the loose shingles, the overgrown weeds, the shuttered windows closing their eyes tight. The sighing porch, down on its knees, begging forgiveness. *What is wrong with these people?* say the neighbors who walk by every day. *What on earth is wrong with the people who live there? Don't they care how it looks? Don't they care that it's falling apart? Look at the cracks in the foundation.*

Look at the rotten boards. Look at the shingles falling out like an old lady's loose teeth.

There is movement in our bedroom. The shadow of Mother's head, a hand, drawing back the corner of the curtain, not enough to see her face, but enough so that she can crouch at the windowsill and peer out at me, ineffectual, impotent, furious, and too afraid to do anything about it. The curtain drops and she moves away.

The rain falls onto the pavement. I stand on the sidewalk and let it cover every inch of me, washing away Mother's stale breath, the whispered voices of guilt and pity, the marvelous hunger of one girl who is brave enough to stretch. I jump in puddles. I twirl and laugh. I open my mouth wide and drink the dark, slick sidewalk, the nighttime sky, the streetlamps, the houses, the trees, and the whole ridiculous, broken world swirling inside of me because it has been mine to drink all along. I close my eyes and allow each drop to touch my face, cool as Daddy's fingertips, bright and unexpected as a prayer.

BLACKBIRD

Trisha Leaver

I loved it there, standing in the shadows, hidden behind the dark velvet curtains, staring at the soundboard. The only place I loved more was the balcony. Littered with spotlights and extra tech crew, the balcony was the one place in the school's auditorium where the public wasn't allowed to sit. The one place where I could stand behind a giant black cylinder and literally shine the spotlight on someone else for a change.

I glanced across the stage, craning my neck to see the stage crew in the left wing. They were mainly seniors trying to complete the mandatory art elective they needed to graduate. Not exactly the most enthusiastic bunch.

The low drone of a voice echoed in my ear, pulling my attention from the glittery costume and overdone facial expressions of Rachel Wilson on stage. The freshman in charge of the lights had screwed up again, missing his cue, and Rachel looked peeved, her eyes narrowing in my direction.

If it were anybody else, I would've torn them a new one, but not Sean Walker. Incompetent or not, Sean was one of the few kids who'd never asked why my brother had opened fire in a crowded school hallway two years ago. Sean never looked at me with the contempt and disgust I'd come to associate with this school. With this town. With everybody I met. And for that reason alone, I gave him one of the coolest jobs.

"Sean." The second I said his name, the light changed position, the bright white hue softening to blue.

"Sorry, Lilly." Sean's voice crackled through my headset. "I got distracted for a minute."

I nodded, completely forgetting that he couldn't see me, then said, "S'okay, but you need to pay better attention."

Everybody got distracted up there their first time. Staring fifty feet down at the seats below, the heat of the bulbs, and the utter darkness that surrounded you were disorienting.

I waited, breath held to make sure Sean hit the next cue, then turned back to the stage. I knew every word to the song Rachel was belting out, could hit every note, transition seamlessly between breaks. Two years ago, that would've been me out there, anchoring the chorus. Two years and four schools back, that *was* me.

Mr. Johnson had called us in early. There was some sort of screwup in the final scene of last night's dress rehearsal. I didn't know exactly what went wrong, just that we all got hauled in early to run through the entire musical again. If four months of rehearsal hadn't beaten the chorus into them, I don't know what Mr. Johnson hoped to accomplish with a before-school practice. Better yet, I didn't know why the tech crew had to be here. With the exception of Sean's minor slipup, we'd done our part damn near perfectly.

I was sitting at the piano in the prop room—more messing around with a bad rendition of Chopsticks than actually playing—as I waited for Mr. Johnson to finish lecturing the cast and get on with the rehearsal. Music seemed to soothe my constant state of anger, and today, I was crankier than usual, probably because of the email I'd accidentally opened this morning. Someone who didn't know me or my family ranting about how my brother was the spawn of Satan. How his evil tendencies were somehow my parents' fault, and how they'd be wise to keep better control of me.

It didn't matter that I'd never so much as gotten anything below a B, or that my mom went to church every morning to pray for the girl my brother had intentionally killed. Our family was marked, our entire life narrowed down to the cruel actions of my brother, James.

"Sixty-eight more days," I whispered to myself. Then I would graduate. Move away. Change my name. Truly start over.

I slammed my fingers down on each key, the sound becoming more musical and less violent as the rage slowly eased from my system. I wished for a safe, quiet place at home where I could take my frustration out on the keys, but our piano hadn't made the move to the tiny, already furnished house we'd rented.

Closing my eyes, I let my fingers dance across the keys, my voice whispering out lyrics I'd long since forgotten. With the play rehearsals, set construction, and wardrobe readjustments occupying every spare inch of this prop room, it'd been weeks since I was able to slip in here unnoticed and lose myself in dreams that no longer existed.

The door opened, and I cursed, letting my hands slap down on the keys, the clash of notes making me wince.

"Sorry. I didn't know anyone was in here."

I stood up from the bench and shook my head. The door was closed, the lights were on, and you could clearly hear the piano. Any idiot would've known someone was in here.

"I'm . . . uh . . . looking for . . ." The boy paused and glanced down at the paper he had nearly crushed in his hand. It was a class schedule, one he obviously hadn't memorized yet. "Mr. Johnson."

I didn't recognize the boy, but that wasn't unusual. It's not like I made a habit out of keeping track of every military brat who transferred in and out of this school.

"Not here," I replied, praying he'd simply turn around and leave.

"Can you tell me where I can find him?" he asked.

I shook my head and responded with a less than helpful, "Nope."

"Okaaay, can you point me in the direction of his office?"

I fanned out my hands in a grand gesture, encompassing everything and nothing. According to Mr. Johnson, this prop room, the stage, and the entire auditorium were his office.

"Will you see him before school starts?" he asked, and I nodded, purposefully staying silent.

"I got put in his Theater Tech class, and I need to talk to him about all the before- and after-school practices he requires."

Theater Tech was an actual class at Pittsfield High School, a forty-five minute slot where we learned the physics of the theater. That class was easy; what irritated my classmates the most was the insane amount of mandatory practices the month before the musical. And from the look on this boy's face, he was no exception.

"I have a note from my parents and the principal getting me out of it." He held out his hand as if the possibility of me not helping him hadn't crossed his mind.

"You're gonna have to find him yourself," I said, smiling. I could hear Mr. Johnson's response already, his rant about how Theater Tech was just as important as English Lit, and he could either show up for practice or take the F.

The boy tucked the note back into his pocket and turned to walk away, pausing at the door. "I'm Adam, by the way. Adam Langley."

I nodded but didn't give him my name, didn't need to. Two hours in this school and someone would fill him in on who I was, or rather who my brother was.

It didn't matter how many new schools I went to or how far away we moved, the rumors and the speculation followed us everywhere. I thought Pittsfield would be different, believed my father when he promised me it would. His logic was sound, infallible. Pittsfield's entire world revolved around the army base. Families constantly moved in and out, a cyclical crop of kids who didn't know me or my family's past. A new opportunity for me to start over, make new friends. Unfortunately, it never worked that way. The few civilian kids here always found a way to fill them in, so every six weeks, I got rejected all over again.

I asked Mom and Dad if we could move again last week when I found another note taped to the windshield of my car in the parking lot. There was another school shooting in Texas, six kids injured, no one killed. The incident prompted a lockdown drill and assembly aimed at instructing us what to do in an armed-intruder situation. It also triggered a slew of vile rumors and steely-eyed glares focused in my direction. I was used to it and shouldn't have let it bother me, but I was having a bad day. And moving again seemed like the easiest solution. My parents shook their heads. We'd run out of places to go. And money.

It took less time for the rumors to spread to Adam than I expected. First period class to be exact. My guess is because he was a boy and an attractive one at that. He went to take the seat next to me in French class only to have Rachel Wilson steer him away. Adam glanced my way a few more times that day, his head cocked as if trying to piece the story together. He could try all he wanted, and it would never make sense. I'd lived through it, asked myself the same insane questions a thousand times, and I still didn't understand, still didn't have answers.

It was opening night, and Mr. Johnson had the entire cast up on stage. He was giving them a last minute pep talk, reminding each person where they screwed up in dress rehearsal. I'd done the same with the tech crew.

I glanced down at my watch. We had forty minutes until showtime. Bored and nervous about letting Sean man the lights, I made my way to the narrow corridor behind the stage to make sure the props were all lined up in the right order. The last thing I needed was everybody screaming at me because of some missing fake rock.

"Sorry I'm late," Adam said, interrupting my highly unorganized mental-cataloging system. "I got hung up at home."

I turned at the sound of his voice, then looked over my shoulder, quite sure he wasn't talking to me. Nobody ever *talked* to me. They talked around me, about me, but never *to* me.

"I thought you had some magic note that got you out of all this," I said.

"I did," Adam replied.

"Then why are you here?"

He shrugged. "Because I have nothing else to do."

His eyes lingered on me until I looked away, heat rising up my neck. What was I . . . some kind of freak show he'd come to watch? The sister of the crazy kid who had shot his girlfriend in the hallway? Not happening. The only entertainment here was on stage.

I swore under my breath and made my way to the storage room in search of the granola bar I'd stuffed in my bag. My last meal was breakfast, and I was already starting to get moody. I knew we'd be here well past eleven tonight, so that rectangle of granola and chocolate chips was my lunch, dinner, and mood-altering snack all rolled into one.

Adam started to follow me. I held up my hand, warning him off. "I'm not interested in anything you have to say," I snapped.

"Umm . . . okay," he said, holding his hands up in mock surrender.

I waited for him to walk away. He didn't; he just stood there, his hands bunched in his pockets, waiting.

"What do you want?" I asked.

He looked around, his eyes skirting over the pulley system used to open and close the curtains. "What do you want me to do? I mean, for Theater Tech."

"You're serious? You want to hang out here with the tech crew?" I asked, and he nodded. "Have you ever worked on a set before?"

"No," he said, shaking his head.

We'd been working as a crew, as a team, for the last four months, each of us the master of our own specific task. We were better organized than the cast, more skilled, too, if you asked me. But Adam, with his impressive two minutes of experience in the technical arts, had the potential to royally screw things up.

"You want to help, then stay out of everybody's way."

A dam had managed to make himself scarce during last night's performance and for that I was grateful. Hopefully he'd take the hint and not come back tonight.

I picked up the paintbrush the prop manager had purposefully left out and started singing along with Rachel as she got in one last early-morning practice with Nathan Reynolds. Some freshman had slammed the rowboat into the wall in a hurry to move it out of the way. The wall would survive, but the giant black mark streaking the side of the boat had to go, and somehow repainting it was my problem.

Nobody could hear me singing. There were two hallways, one closed door, and a thick set of velvet curtains between me and the stage, but the hushed tones of the melody still filtered in, soft enough for my voice to carry over Rachel's in the tiny shop room I was working in.

Nathan was great, but I'd pretty much expected that when I'd heard he'd scored a full ride to Berkeley. Our voices blended together in perfect harmony, whereas Rachel's voice was forced, tense. I was better. But to be fair, I'd performed her part as a freshman, back in a town and a school where I was no longer welcome. So maybe it was more practice than raw talent that had me smiling inwardly as I sang.

My voice fell flat when I felt the soft brush of air drift through the room. Someone had opened the door to the shop room and was listening to me.

"What do you want?" I asked, my face seven shades of red as I stared up at Adam. "I thought I told you to stay out of my way."

"You did, but Mr. Johnson said I could only pass his class if I have a real function. Assigned by you. Plus the one thing that will piss my father off more than me taking Theater Tech is me pulling out an A in a class he thinks is girly."

I quickly looked around the room for something he could do, a task that preferably needed to be done outside. Finding nothing, I tossed him a paintbrush, figuring painting was one thing he couldn't mess up. We worked in silence for a few minutes, me carefully waiting until his brush had cleared the can before dipping mine in. No intentional interaction; no conversation. I'd learned that trick a long time ago. Keep people out, make it clear you have no interest in talking to them, and they will leave you alone. Blissfully, agonizingly alone.

The pianist—Mr. Johnson's wife—bridged into the next ballad. Rachel stumbled to make the transition, and I instinctively filled in where her words dropped off. I had finished that song and hummed the chorus to the next when Adam finally asked, "Why are you back here?" He waved his hands to encompass the dark, musty-smelling shop room. "Instead of out there singing?"

"Not good enough," I said, hoping he'd swallow my lie and let it go. No use explaining to him that since my brother's violent psychotic break, I spent my days avoiding attention rather than seeking it out.

Adam laughed, a full-on howl that had me itching to smack him. "Yeah, I've been here a total of two days and even I know that it isn't Rachel's voice that's carrying her."

I smiled, cursing myself as I did. But he was right. It didn't matter that Rachel sounded more like a bad lounge singer than a practiced soprano. Her insane popularity meant most girls avoided going up against her, helping her land the part by default, not on merit.

"I don't see you out there singing," I fired back.

"Can't carry a tune," Adam replied, tossing his paintbrush aside. He held his hand out to help me up. When I didn't take it he reached down and grabbed on to my shoulders, hauled me to my feet, then nudged me toward the door. "Follow me."

A dam led me into the prop room where he'd caught me playing yesterday morning. He shut the door behind us, locking me in and everybody else out, then made his way over to the piano and ran his fingers lightly across the keys as if testing their resistance. He played a few scales, wincing as the age and disrepair of the piano whined back at him.

"You play?" I said, asking the obvious. I don't know why it surprised me. Maybe because he was tall and athletic. Maybe because the first time I met him, he was trying to get out of anything remotely related to the school musical.

"I do," he said as he depressed the left pedal, hitting two strings instead of three. It didn't have much effect—the piano was older than this school—but I got his point nonetheless. Not only could he play, but he was good. Damn good.

"You can blame my mad piano skills on my mom. She insisted I learn, convinced my father that mastering a musical instrument would provide me with the discipline necessary to become a man of honor."

"Man of honor?" I repeated. It was an interesting term, one that didn't have much place in this school.

"Yeah, my father didn't buy it either so Mom snuck me there every Wednesday while he was overseeing drills." Adam stopped playing and stood up, the piano bench scraping across the floor as he bowed. "Adam Langley the fourth. First and only son of General Adam Langley the third, current commander of Pittsfield Army Base, and Congressional Medal of Honor recipient."

I laughed. It was inappropriate, and rude, and completely unnecessary, but the sarcasm in his voice, the way his nose scrunched up in distaste as he recited his father's merits was just plain old amusing. "And you have no desire to follow in his footsteps no matter what he wants."

"Uh . . . no. I'm the kid more likely to mow down your mailbox on the way home from a party than rise to the rank of general in the army."

I thought back to Saturday morning and the rather vile curse that I woke to as my father stood on the front lawn, scooping up mail. Our mailbox had been smashed into a million pieces, the wooden post lying in the middle of the road.

Adam caught the way my eyes drifted, a small smile lighting

my face as my memory dialed back a few days. "Crap . . . that was your mailbox?"

"It was."

"I'll pay for it," he quickly said. "Or my dad will. Or maybe the army. I don't know, but it doesn't matter. I will fix it myself. After school. Today. Promise."

"No worries," I said. I didn't care about the mailbox; better him than the vandals who frequented our street, spray-painting our front lawn and shouting obscenities as they drove by.

"Play me something," I said. I don't know why I asked, but something about him put me at ease, made me feel happy in a world . . . in a *school* that hated me.

"Sing me something," he countered.

I shook my head. He could show off all he wanted, but I had no intention of joining in. "So your dad wants you to be in the military like him?" I asked, trying to deflect the conversation off me and back onto him.

"Yep," Adam said, his fingers not missing a single note as he spoke. "Like him. And my grandfather. And his father before that."

"You going to?" I asked, oddly excited that somebody else struggled with a past, a set of dreams and obligations that weren't his. It made him more real. And since I understood miserable and flawed, it made my life seem less impossible.

"Not if I have my way," Adam said.

The musical lasted one week, and every night it seemed like some incompetent idiot managed to break some part of the set. Each morning, I'd find myself back in the shop room, a handsaw, a paintbrush, and a bad attitude in hand. Every time, Adam would walk in smiling and humming some stupid Beatles song.

It took him five days to get up the courage to ask me about my brother, and even then it seemed more curiosity than anything else. No judgment, no misplaced assumption that I was as crazy as James. Only a *Hey, you know all about my insanely controlling dad, so now it is your turn to tell me about your insanely messed-up brother.*

"So your brother . . . is what they say about him true?"

I shrugged, feigning disinterest. He'd heard it all; the gossip network in this school was intact and thriving. "Depends on what they're saying."

"Did he really kill all those kids?"

"No, just one and then himself," I said, cringing at how callous I sounded. One was enough. One was too many.

I held my breath, waiting for the usual onslaught of questions. The administration at my old high school, the police, my parents, crap, even the national news had all verbalized concerns. Did we see it coming? Was James screwed up to begin with? Was there a history of mental illness in our family? How did he get the gun? Those questions had been asked and answered a thousand times, but they never went away, never stopped plaguing my every thought.

"No. No. No. And who the hell knows," I bit out, preempting Adam's questions.

He cocked his head, genuinely confused by my suddenly pissy attitude. "Ooookay."

"I'm sorry. It's not you, it's—"

"No, I totally get that you don't want to talk about it."

That wasn't it. I did want to talk about it, wanted to pour out my fears to somebody who I knew wouldn't judge me or post my answers on the Internet for the entire world to see. I just never expected it to be Adam.

"He was a senior; I was only a freshman," I started, recalling a story I'd buried away and yet remembered every second of every day. "He was going to LSU to play ball. He'd gotten his award letter that afternoon, but it wasn't enough. Even with the scholarship, my parents were tens of thousands of dollars short. James was upset, scared about how and *if* my parents would be able to come up with the rest of the money. All he had was baseball. And Kim."

Adam nodded, his small smile encouraging me to keep talking, to open up and let somebody in for the first time ever. "He skipped practice that afternoon and went over to Kim's house like he always did when he was upset. She was there; so was his best friend Nick. They were . . . umm . . . You know."

"Got it," he said when I trailed off. "But it happened at school, not at Kim's house, right?"

"Yep." I paused, remembering the one detail that still haunted me, the one tiny detail that made me feel like somehow I could've stopped this.

"James made me take the bus that day. Since the day he got his license, he'd always driven me to school, even stayed after when I had chorus practice so he could drive me home. But that morning, he insisted I take the bus. I swore at him, told him he was being a prick for no reason, and just because Mom and Dad weren't rich enough to pay for college didn't mean he could be a jerk to me. And then I left, didn't even think twice that something could be off."

"None of that was your fault, Lilly," Adam said, reading my tone for what it was—guilt.

"I know," I lied. "He took a bat to Nick's head, leaving him for dead." Nobody thought twice about him walking around the school with a bat. Since he was the captain of the baseball team, they probably figured he'd come from the batting cage in the field house.

"I don't know where he got the gun." I continued, "He shot Kim, then killed himself. I saw him do it. I was standing at my locker, five down from hers. I begged him not to do it, but it's like he didn't see me . . . didn't even know me."

"Nick?" Adam questioned.

I smiled, Nick was the only bright spot in all of this. I'd talked to him two weeks ago. He'd called from college. It was my brother's birthday, and he wanted to see how I was doing. Of all the people in the world, Nick had the most reason to hate my family, to blame us for not seeing some sign that truly wasn't there. But he didn't.

"He's a sophomore at UNC," I finally said.

"And you're stuck here, hiding out behind the stage, gluing a set back together."

I reached for the hammer and pounded an unnecessary nail into the fake rock wall that Rachel had complained was wobbly and unsafe. "Yep." It didn't matter how far we moved or how many years went by; there were some pasts you couldn't escape.

W hen was the last time you really sang?" Adam asked. It was the last night of the school musical, and I'd given him the menial job of opening and closing the curtains. He kept staring at his watch and shuffling his feet like he was irritated that I didn't trust him with something more substantial. He'd been painting and repairing pieces of the set with me each morning before school, so in his mind, surely he was competent enough to run the soundboard. Truth was, I wanted to be around him and assigning him a less techy thing to do meant he had more downtime to spend with me.

"Solo night is tomorrow," Adam added, and I motioned for him to stop talking and pay attention. The first act was over, and he'd yet to close the curtain. He yanked on the pulley, the heavy blue velvet stuttering its way across the stage. I laughed; easiest job in the world, and somehow he'd managed to botch it.

He waited for the crowd of sweaty cast members to pass before he leaned in and whispered again. "There are thirteen of them singing tomorrow."

I nodded, my attention split between his useless chatter and the costume director screaming in my ear about a stack of hatboxes I hadn't seen, never mind moved. I'd worry about solo night sometime tomorrow, after the missing hat crisis was over. Besides, Mr. Johnson had already given me the lineup, and I'd passed it on to the crew. It was a no-brainer for us. All we had to do was check the sound and shine one spotlight on each of the soloists as they sang. It was more of an ego-stroking event than an actual musical performance.

"You don't have to be here if you already have plans," I said, giving Adam an easy out. Half the kids in Theater Tech had managed to weasel their way out of working solo night. Can't say I blamed them. It was the first Saturday night in weeks that they weren't required to be here for practice. Only the unpopular volunteered to work that night. The unpopular and me.

"We can pretty much handle it with three people," I said.

"Nope, I'm planning on being here. You?"

"Kind of have to," I said. Solo night was open to anybody in the school's chorus, a chance for them to show off their talent. They picked a song, Mr. Johnson arranged the accompaniment, and the tech crew, aka me, oversaw the lights and the soundboard.

Most people chose one song; Rachel was doing three. She'd specifically requested a change in hue for the second of her three solo performances. Apparently a tinge of pink was exactly what she needed to take her voice from bearable to simply mediocre. According to her, since I didn't have a boyfriend, friends, or any life to speak of, I should be the one to personally oversee the culmination of her high school musical career.

"I'll let you run the lights." I giggled, already envisioning Adam trying to figure them out with little to no instruction. It'd be amusing, more so for me than for Rachel Wilson, but that was kind of the point.

"I know exactly what you are thinking and stop." He chuckled. "I have no desire to mess up Rachel's performance. I'm curious to know who's in charge up there, that's all."

"Sean, I think, why?"

"No reason," he replied and turned his attention back to the stage, starting to hum that same stupid song he'd been picking out on the piano this past week as I worked. I'd hum the words out, even got caught singing a couple of embarrassing times, but it was getting to the point where I hated that stupid song and wondered if it was the only one he could play.

Thirteen singers, fifteen songs. It was nine forty-five and the lyrics, the melody, even the singers' damn names were starting to blur together. If it hadn't been for Adam's running commentary on Rachel's three costume changes, I would've packed it in a long time ago, tossed the headset aside and left Sean in charge of the entire production.

"Last one," I mumbled into my headset. There was a kid from the AV club running the soundboard, something about digitally recording the event so they could make some money selling copies to parents. I didn't care, so long as they didn't break anything.

I turned around, curious as to why Adam had suddenly gone silent, only to find he wasn't there. I spun in a complete circle, figuring one of the soloists—Rachel in particular—had pulled him aside. I found Rachel and her permanent sidekick, Angela, but not Adam.

He'd been acting strange all night, nervous and jumpy. I'd asked him a few times if he needed to leave, if he had plans or, more likely, an irate father waiting for him at home. Each time Adam assured me that he was fine, just anxious to make sure everything went exactly as planned. I wasn't sure why; it was my neck on the line if something went wrong backstage, not his.

Wondering if he'd taken me up on my sarcastic offer to run the lights, I stupidly squinted up at the balcony, blinding myself. The spotlight went dark, the audience rising to their feet in a thunderous roar of applause. Nathan had just finished, and even I had to admit his performance warranted that reaction.

I slid my headset off, letting it cradle my neck. I had no right to be pissed at Adam for slipping away. I had no claim to him, not even as a friend. Sure, he'd helped me paint a few sets while he racked up the necessary brownie points to score an A in Theater

Tech. I mean, if I was really being honest with myself, his impromptu morning piano sessions were nothing more than him amusing himself as I did most of the work. I knew all that, had logically figured it out the second morning when I found myself uncomfortably excited to see him, yet I refused to believe it. It was nice to finally hope, to have somebody to hang around with, to think someone could look at me and, for once, not see the shadow of my brother.

The headset caught in my braid, and I yanked hard, taking a chunk of my hair out with it. "You good to finish up?" I spoke into the microphone, tossing the headset aside before Sean even had a chance to answer. Regardless, I was outta here.

My coat was in the prop room, tossed on top of the piano bench. I toyed with sitting down and playing, taking my anger and frustration, my hatred for life out on the ivory keys. But leave it to Adam and this school to ruin the one thing I had left— music.

The halls were getting crowded, cries of "congratulations" and "you were amazing" filtering into the room. I cursed the tears streaming down my cheeks; it was my own stupid fault for caring . . . for hoping.

"You're an idiot," I mumbled as I curled myself into the dark corner of that room, praying I would just simply disappear.

The music drifted through the hall, soft and muted, and for the first time, in tune. It was that stupid Beatles song Adam had taken to playing—"Blackbird." And if my ears were right, he was sitting dead center stage, playing the piano none of us were allowed to touch. The only piano in this entire school that was tuned regularly.

The entire auditorium was dark, but I wasn't surprised. I'd been hiding out in that room for over twenty minutes, waiting for the place to clear out. I took a step onto the stage, my eyes instinctively scanning the first few rows of seats. Without lights, I couldn't see anything, was literally trusting Adam's music to guide my feet.

"What are you doing?" I asked as my hand grazed the piano. "Mr. Johnson will kill you if he sees you playing that."

"Sing for me, Lilly." He must have sensed my hesitation, the way I looked around for people I knew weren't there, because his fingers softened on the keys, pleading right alongside his words. "Sing for *me*."

He morphed the bridge he was playing back to the beginning, had to play the same string of notes three times before I got up the courage to whisper out the first few words. Even then, they were choppy, stuck in my throat.

Adam circled back, and I knew what he was doing—instructing me to start over, to find my voice . . . to find my courage, forget everything, and simply sing.

Blackbird singing in the dead of night.
Take these broken wings and learn to fly.

There was rustling in the balcony, and I knew instantly that I wasn't alone, that darkness didn't make things disappear, it only hid them, and even then, only for a short while.

I turned to run off the stage, a hand—Adam's hand—grabbing my wrist. He squeezed harder when I tried to yank it free, pulling me down until I was sitting next to him on the bench. "Sing. For. *Me*," he repeated as if his voice alone could make me forget that someone was up in that balcony, watching me.

When I stayed silent, Adam started singing. With the piano to drown out his voice, Adam was bad. But singing a cappella, like he was now, he was awful.

"You really suck," I said, and he laughed but kept right on singing.

"That he does," Mr. Johnson said. "And I have a very strict don't-touch-my-piano rule." He motioned for us to get up, then sat down and adjusted the small light that illuminated the sheets of music. He began to play . . . same song, same gentle whisper of notes that Adam had started.

Adam hummed the first chorus, whispered the words to the second into my ear, his hand squeezing mine as he willed me to find my voice. The spotlight above flared to life, shining only on Mr. Johnson at the piano, leaving me blissfully in the dark. I could see his face, his whispered words of encouragement as he played the same chorus over and over, waiting, daring me to sing.

"It is just me, him, and Sean," Adam promised. "Trust me on this, just sing."

I did. I closed my eyes, the words barely escaping my throat. I blocked everything out: Sean listening to me from the balcony, Mr. Johnson sitting at the piano playing a song I knew by heart, even the feel of Adam's hand locked in mine. All there was was me, the wooden stage beneath my feet, and the overwhelming feeling of finally being free.

I don't remember hitting the last note or Adam picking me up and swinging me around. But I do remember the deafening silence that hit me when I finished. Sean turned on the lights, and I dug deep, found the strength to open my eyes.

The first clap came from the balcony, echoing through the auditorium with the force of an impending storm. It was Sean, the way he yelled out my name giving him away. An eternally long second passed. Then Mr. Johnson joined in, rising to his feet.

"So you've been in this school for a little over five months," Mr. Johnson said as he made his way over to us. "Hiding your talent, tucked behind the stage with the tech crew, leaving me to suffer through performance after performance with Rachel Wilson."

I nodded. That sounded about right. "I don't sing," I lied, and he nearly doubled over in laughter, Adam joining him.

"She sings all right," Adam choked out. "And she's done hiding from everybody, including herself."

GONE FROM THIS PLACE

Faith Erin Hicks

THE SWEETER THE SIN
Jordan Sonnenblick

So, there was this girl I met on the first day of freshman year at my high school in the city. We had four classes together over the four years of high school. Biology. Chemistry. Poetry. History. I was so hot for her from the very beginning that it was nearly supernatural. Maybe, looking back on it, she was that hot for me, as well, but I don't really think so. I am going to estimate that she was between 57 and 83 percent as attracted to me as I was to her.

But hey, if I'd known that for sure at the time, it would have been good enough for me. It's amazing what the combination of high testosterone and low self-esteem will do to a guy's expectations.

Right before I met the girl (Elizabeth. Her name was Elizabeth. Still is. She's not freaking dead or anything. This isn't that kind of story.), I had spent two weeks training for soccer season at a college campus upstate. That mattered because, well, speaking of high testosterone, I had been cooped up nonstop with fifty guys in a run-down, crappy dorm, listening to their caveman ideas about high-school women.

All the junior and senior guys talked about—and remember,

these were the varsity players, the ones the coaches told us eleven times before breakfast were "the men you want to become!"—was sex. They didn't talk about love or romance or dating. They talked about sex. They rated girls. No, they rated bodies, graded them, classified them. (There were no charts or graphs, but there might as well have been.) They specifically talked about girls as bodies, like, "I would so jump up on that body!" and "I had that body!" and "I'm'a get that body!"

My parents had never, ever talked about sex with me—still haven't, really. Once, when I was about to head out to a big party sophomore year, my dad took me aside and asked, "Son, you know about, uh . . ."

He looked like he was going to die of embarrassment, and I know I felt like I might, too, so I mumbled, "Yeah, I'm good," and that was the end of my training in the finer points of relationship building.

Which was probably just as well, seeing as how Mom was going to dump Dad's ass without any warning the summer before junior year. Dad didn't see it coming. I didn't see it coming. I still don't really understand what happened. All I know is that if obliviousness with females is a genetically acquired trait, my parents' situation would explain a lot about my own.

Come to think of it, even if it's an environmentally acquired trait, I'm still screwed. Meanwhile, Dad's learning how to live on microwaveable dinners, and Mom's living in a deluxe apartment uptown with her boss.

Anyway, I had no home training, and I hung out with a bunch of animal jocks. I had no clue how to get a girl, or how to treat her if I somehow did manage to get her. I didn't even know what "getting" a girl would exactly entail. Would we hang out at cafés and have lively discussions about literature over lattes, or would it be basically all me having and getting and jumping on that body?

Hey, I was up for anything.

But Elizabeth. Wow. She was the kind of girl who was too pretty, too sexual for me to actually talk to in person as though she were a person, if you know what I mean. Basically, looking back on it, I flirted with her by insulting her all through bio class every day, because if I had tried to open up and be serious, I would have gotten all flustered and had nothing to say.

Because I was a dorky little freshman with braces, and she was smoking hot. She had poise. She was three inches taller than I was. She was from a much more sophisticated neighbourhood She outweighed me, for God's sake, and the weight was distributed in endlessly fascinating ways. So I mocked her.

No, that line of thought doesn't make any sense in retrospect, but it's what I went with. We dueled and fenced our way through freshman year. She sat in the row in front of me, immediately to my right, in class. This one time I remember, we were dissecting fetal pigs, and she turned and asked me whether she was supposed to cut just the skin off of her pig's legs, or cut deeper.

Sarcastically, I said, "Nah, just chop the whole extremity right the hell off." In my defense, we had step-by-step notes in front of us, and there was a PowerPoint with diagrams on a tablet for every row of seats in the room. But the next thing I heard was a sickening *crunch*.

The teacher came running over and barked, "Elizabeth, what in the world did you do to that specimen?"

I couldn't resist. I leaned forward and said, "I'm going to go out on a limb here, and say she pushed a little too hard with her scalpel."

Elizabeth flashed me a look of pure rage. She looked kind of steamy when her face got flushed like that. There's something so . . . erotic . . . about an angry girl with surgical tools who's just mistakenly dismembered a gestational hog. Or maybe it was just the seductive scent of formaldehyde wafting through the air.

Then, this one Saturday night, about a third of the way through the year, my parents threw a dinner party, and my best friend, Jeremy, came along with his parents. Jeremy and I were supposed to stay in my room, but at some point, we snuck downstairs to the basement, where the bottles of booze were lined up. We just meant to sneak a few swigs, but I guess a few swigs provided enough alcohol to do the trick, considering I probably weighed about a hundred and two pounds at the time. Counting my sneakers, watch, keys, and phone.

Ah, my phone. After we completed the daring ninja mission of returning to my bedroom without our parents busting us, I decided it would be a brilliant idea to call Elizabeth and declare my undying love to her.

I might have been a bit sketchy on the precise definition of *love* at that point in the evening. Or, you know, in general.

Jeremy tried to wrestle the phone away from me. I mean, he really tried. I don't remember the details, but I do know that my room got pretty trashed, and my phone screen was cracked when I woke up in the morning.

But true love prevailed!

Love, lust, whatever.

That's how I found myself on the phone with an extremely furious Papa Elizabeth, who made clear several key facts to me:

1. Elizabeth had gone to bed, and left her phone on the hall table of their apartment. (I was like, *Who goes to bed this early?*)
2. I was calling after one in the morning. (I was like, *Ah, scratch that last thing I said.*)
3. He didn't know who I was, or what I was thinking. (I was like, *Dude. Who's thinking?*)
4. I had some serious explaining to do. (*Yeah, I'm getting that.*)
5. His daughter did not waste her precious time hanging out with lowlife boys like me. (*Oh, yeah? Well, uh . . .*)

But I was not to be deterred. I don't know what I said, but there must have been pleading involved, and also claims of emergency status. And then—yay!—Elizabeth got on the phone.

"David?"

"Uh, yes, sir. Ma'am. E-lizzy."

"Why in the world are you calling me at one forty-three in the morning?"

"I dunno. I miss you. And, uh, your face. And stuff. And the talks we have. You know."

"What are you talking about? We don't have talks. You make fun of me. And then you trick me into mangling dead piglets. How is that 'talks'? Oh, my God. Are you drunk?"

I was horrified. I remember thinking my parents were going to hear her. "Sssshhhhh!" I whispered as loudly as I could. Spit flew all over Jeremy, who was lying on the floor next to me, literally gasping with laughter.

"You *are* drunk!" Then her voice changed. Suddenly, she sounded kind of triumphant. "Hah! You might laugh at me all the time, but I'm the girl you call when you're drunk. Good night, David. Sweet dreams . . ."

And then she was gone. And then I was crawling to the bathroom. And then Jeremy somehow disappeared. And it was morning. The sun was too bright. My phone was broken.

And it was Monday. And I couldn't look Elizabeth in the eye. But she couldn't stop smirking at me.

Sophomore year, in chem class, we teased each other back and forth basically nonstop. Sometimes I hated her; sometimes she hated me. But always—always—I couldn't wait to see her when she walked in. I wanted to see how she looked, what she was wearing, whether she was smiling. And then when she inevitably caught me looking, I never, ever started any kind of human conversation.

Then one day, I was deeply involved in a lab experiment, and Elizabeth asked me, "Is this the gas jet or the water spigot? It's the gas jet, right?" Because for some incredibly stupid reason, all the gas-jet attachments in our labs looked exactly the same as the water taps. It was just an accident waiting to happen, if you ask me. A liability nightmare.

I wasn't looking, okay? I was busy. I was involved in my work. Plus, Elizabeth was wearing a flowy dress and she was standing really close and she smelled really good and I couldn't handle being so close to her. I said, "Yeah," without even thinking about it.

Then there was this *fwoosh!* noise, and water was everywhere. Apparently, Elizabeth had hooked up the rubber tubing for a Bunsen burner to one of the water spigots, and then cranked that thing up. The water had gone shooting through the tubing, straight up through the burner, and all the way up to the ceiling of the classroom, before splattering all over everything within maybe a ten-foot radius.

So the chem teacher came over and started yelling at Elizabeth, who said, "But David *told* me it was the gas jet!"

The teacher asked, "David, is this true?" I couldn't answer. First of all, I was laughing so hard I couldn't breathe. Second, Elizabeth's dress was soaked, and clinging to her all over, I was afraid I might faint if I tried to say anything, but I finally choked out something about how I hadn't been paying attention.

After class, she came up to me in the hall, poked me in the chest, and said, "So, was that really an accident? Or did you just want to see what I look like when I'm all wet?"

Junior year. Poetry. Our teacher, Miss Hawk, was obsessed with two things: haiku and 1980s song lyrics. I hated poetry with a burning passion. I had signed up for a short-story class, with drama as my second choice. You had to put a third choice on the form, so I had randomly put poetry on there. Elizabeth loved poetry, though. For the first time, I realized she was incredibly smart and funny and talented. Now I was the one who kept making mistakes.

I mean, mine didn't cause any lab catastrophes, but there were all sorts of poetical failures going on. It was like I was still figuring out how to hold a crayon, while she was seriously *composing*.

I still remember my best haiku:

Flying through the air,
They sparkle in the sunlight.
Dazzling flying fish!

And Elizabeth's:

It takes just one look,
A skin on skin, a sparking,
A brush and a breath.

Elizabeth never said anything directly. Why would she have to? She just smiled and shined, except in one area. Miss Hawk loved bringing in audio clips for us to listen to, especially old recordings of poetry readings and her beloved 1980s pop songs. One day, she had us try to transcribe some of the poetry in small groups, and I realized that my ear was better than Elizabeth's. Elizabeth had a lot of trouble distinguishing what the poets were saying, especially if there was background noise in the recordings. I didn't make a big deal of it, because I knew she was so much better at actually writing and understanding poems than I was, and also because maybe—maybe—I was starting to learn something.

And then we had a lesson about an ancient band called U2. There was a line in one of their songs that went, "Sweet the sin, but bitter the taste in my mouth." Of course, Miss Hawk wanted to go on and on about the deeper meaning, but Elizabeth leaned against me (yes, by this point I realized we had chosen to sit near each other in every class) and whispered in my ear, "Doesn't it say, 'The sweeter the sin, the better the taste in my mouth'?"

She was totally wrong about the lyric, but I didn't care. Her breath was on my ear, her body was pressed up to mine, and her voice had that same tone I remembered, dreamlike, from my drunk-dialed freshman-year phone call.

I managed to gasp, "I'm not sure, but it probably should."

When the bell rang for the next period, I had to sit there for a few minutes to calm down after everyone else left.

Senior year, in history, there wasn't even any question of where we would sit. Our teacher, Mr. Romanescu, was a real winner: he weighed about three hundred pounds; he wore these bizarre sweat-dress-pants every day with a dress shirt unbuttoned at the top and several gold chains around his neck; and he was always sweating like a horse after a big race. Oh, and he had huge mut-tonchop sideburns, plus a handlebar mustache, which gave him the air of a pimp from a really old movie.

The first day, Elizabeth slipped into the seat to my right. When Mr. Romanescu waddled in, she purred under her breath, "Ooh, baby! Come to mama!"

How I loved that class. Mr. Romanescu actually knew his sub-ject, but his grammar was awful. He would say things like, "If you was George Washington, what would you have done at Valley

Forge?" Elizabeth would tap me on the leg, and say, "You think he minored in English?" I'd whisper back, "Nah, personal hygiene. But you was close."

In March that year, we ended up at a party together. She had been in the cast of a play, and I had been in the pit band. After closing night, someone somehow rented a big, empty loft. There were kegs lined up along one wall, with piles and piles of big, red plastic cups. We were both drinking. Somehow, when the dancing started, even though the room was packed, Elizabeth and I kept ending up next to each other, in front of each other, back-to-back. And—unless I was crazy—at some point, Elizabeth started leaning into me. I couldn't figure it out. We hadn't been dancing with each other, per se. There had been other partners. There might have even been groups.

There had certainly been groups of beers going down my throat.

But there we were, pressed up against a wall. Elizabeth looked up at me and said, "Hey, you used to be shorter than me!"

I said, "Not anymore." Because, you know, genius of wit.

Then she said, "That lyric totally should have been, 'The sweeter the sin, the better the taste in my mouth.' Am I right?"

Continuing to hold up my end of the conversation, I said, "Uh." I wanted to say yes. I wanted to agree with everything she ever said, forevermore. But what came out was, "Uh."

She grabbed my hand, and said, "I'll *show* you."

I had told my parents I was going to sleep at a friend's house, which I somehow miraculously remembered. I said, "Wait, my ride."

She followed me through the packed dance floor—*we were holding hands!*—until I found my friend and told him I had new plans. He grinned and said, "Yeah, I feel you. Just be careful."

I was like, *What can possibly go wrong?*

Then Elizabeth took control. She pulled me by the hand down a bunch of flights of stairs until we hit the cold air of the downtown street, and then we walked until we found an alarming-looking alley.

If I had been sober, I would have been dragging Elizabeth in any other direction, because I have seen the Batman movies. I know what happens in deserted downtown alleyways in the small hours of morning. I wanted to fool around with a girl, not have a mugger jump out and shoot our mommies and daddies.

But I was not sober. So, when Elizabeth plunged her hands into my hair and used her hips to press me back against the wall of the alley, I ignored the little *ping!* of danger that was ringing in the back of my mind, and the louder *gong!* sound as my shoulders slammed against a metal sign riveted to the bricks behind me. And when she kissed me until I couldn't breathe, and my heart pounded so hard I thought she must be able to feel it through both of our thin, insufficient jackets, and she said, "See? The sweeter the sin, the better the taste in my mouth," all I could say was, "Yeah, yes, *yes!*"

We were there for a long, strange time, doing things just a few feet away from the street that I'd never done before with anybody else. Nobody was out but a few staggering homeless people, and a few—much scarier—loud, boisterous groups of teen gangsters. At one point, I was pretty sure I heard a young man's voice shouting, "Yeah, baby! Get some!"

Elizabeth and I inched farther into the dark of the alley. I ignored, or mostly ignored, the damp of the dew forming on the metal behind my head, the shouts of the teenagers passing within ten feet of us as our hands roamed, the mulch of trash and puddle water underfoot, and anything else except the pulse at Elizabeth's throat, the rush of my breath, the steam of hers.

And then, at some point, when the street was as quiet as a cathedral and my lips and loins felt bruised and dull, we both sort of woke up, pulled away, and looked at each other.

"We, uh . . ." she said.

"I should get you to a cab," I said, my longest and most coherent sentence of the evening.

Without another word, we straightened the outer layers of our clothing, smiled shyly at each other, and stepped gingerly out of the alley. We were only about four blocks from a main street, where there were taxis running even at that hour. I held out my arm, and the very first one pulled over.

"Well, that was fun," she said, with that wicked note I now recognized.

I reached in past her and handed a wad of money to the cab driver. As I went to pull back out, I looked at her from about two inches away, and tried to think of something to say, but it was as though I had gone back to freshman year.

I stepped back from the curb, and the cab left. I checked my pockets and realized I had given the cabbie all of my money. It was a twenty-five-block walk to my friend's apartment, and he wasn't expecting me, but my house was even farther away, plus there was no way I'd be able to explain it if I showed up on foot, reeking of alcohol and whatever else I'd leaned against or stepped in.

I started the long, scary slog uptown. My legs ached. Everything below my waist throbbed with every step. I hoped the gangs had called it a night, because I was too wasted to run.

There was a bitter taste in my mouth.

I texted my friend from the lobby of his building, and his phone woke him up. He buzzed me in, and it was basically all good.

I didn't get shot.

I didn't get stabbed.

Elizabeth didn't get raped or killed.

But the next morning, I woke up feeling vaguely disgusted with myself. My friend let me take the first shower, but I had to put on the same clothes again. In the light of day, the back of each piece of clothing wasn't pretty. And then I had to beg my friend for subway fare. I mean, he gave it to me, but it was just more proof of how stupid the whole thing had been, and how lucky I was to be getting home safely.

That was when I thought of Elizabeth.

I texted her in a panic. After the longest eleven minutes of my life, she wrote back, "Why are you always waking me up? ☺"

But, you know, I still couldn't talk with her that Monday. Eventually, I got up the nerve to ask her out on an actual date, and the weirdest thing happened: we became friends. And *then* I couldn't make a move, because it was somehow too late. We went back to her apartment, and talked until super late, and laughed through all our years of history together.

It was strangely terrible to find I'd done it all so ass-backwards. This was a girl I could have really liked, if I hadn't *liked* her so much. If I hadn't started out so transparently obsessed with having and getting and jumping on her body.

We went out two more times, and the same thing happened: great talk, great laughs, and not even a good-night kiss. It was all messed up, it was all out of order—and I didn't know how to even begin to fix it. I had no *game*.

And then another guy asked her to the prom, and she said yes.

Tomorrow we graduate. I'm sitting here at a party, *not* drinking, maybe fifty feet away from Elizabeth, who's leaning back against her prom date. I notice she's also staying far, far from the alcohol. Maybe she's doing some reflecting, too. Today was the day when we all wrote in one another's yearbooks, and Elizabeth wrote this in mine: "Somewhere under the definition of SAGA in the dictionary, there is a picture of you & me."

And damn, it's true. But I blew the whole thing, so I am trying to figure out what I've learned, because next year I'll be a freshman again. I might meet another Elizabeth.

Nah, there will never be another Elizabeth.

But now I know that a beautiful girl, a poetic girl, a plunging-her-hands-through-my-hair girl, just might be attracted to me, if I don't blow it by being obnoxious, or by choking instead of opening up. Or by getting drunk and being dangerously stupid.

So I guess the question is, will I be smart enough to learn from all of this biology, chemistry, poetry, and history?

Elizabeth winks at me from across the room. She actually *winks*.

I don't know whether I'll be smart enough. But at least now I know it's possible.

THE MISTAKE

James Preller

1

"What do you think we should do?" Angela asked.

"I don't know." Malcolm shook his head. "What do *you* want?"

It was, he thought, the right thing to ask. A reasonable question. Her choice. Besides, the truth was, he didn't want to say *it* out loud.

So he said the thing he said.

"What do I want?" Angela said, as if shocked, as if hearing the ridiculous words for the first time. She stared at her skinny, dark-haired boyfriend and spat out words like lightning bolts, like thunder. "What's that got to do with anything, Mal? What I *want*? How can you even ask me that?"

"I'm sorry," he said.

"I'm sorry, too," she replied stiffly, but Angela's *sorry* seemed different from his. Malcolm was sorry for the mistake they made. Their carelessness. And in all honesty, his *sorry* in this conversation was also a strategy to silence her, a word that acted like a spigot to turn off the anger. Angela's *sorry* encompassed the whole wide world that now rested on her slender shoulders. Malcolm understood that she was sorry for all of it, all the world's weary sorrows, and most especially for the baby that was growing inside her belly.

2

Angela on her cell, punching keys, scrolling, reading, clicking furiously.

At Planned Parenthood, there was a number she could text. She sent a question. Then another. And another.

She was trying to be brave.

Trying so hard.

It wasn't working out so well.

3

"Why are you looking at that shit now?" he said. "Everybody's waiting at the park."

"You don't care anyway," she replied, and pocketed the phone in a way that just broke his heart in half.

Really? he thought. *We're doing this now?*

Girls and their drama. He wasn't up for it, wasn't down with it, didn't want any part of it. Suddenly there was such a fierce fire in her eyes, blinding, like the noon sun's reflection off still water.

It wasn't so much the *look* in her eyes. People say that, but it doesn't describe real life. Nobody sees someone's eyes from across the room, like in some dumb book—"she shot daggers with her eyes." *Uh-huh, yeah, right.* That's not what he saw that day. What happened was Angela's face ignited like a torch, not just her eyes, but her nose and cheeks and mouth and chin, all of it, the whole thing—fierce as a warehouse fire. Then at once her face shattered like a smashed mirror, and every shard registered a new emotion: anger, hope, fear, sorrow, betrayal, love, and on and on and on.

Freaking girls, man.

The guys were waiting for him, probably pissed, probably starting a game without him. *Who's gonna play point guard? Teddy? Ha, that's a joke, he's got no handle. A shoot-first guy, not a distributor.*

Seeing all this, thinking these things, Malcolm said in a soft voice, "Angie, baby, what the fuck?"

And damn if that wasn't the wrong thing to ask. Everything he said nowadays was a mistake. He already missed how things used to be.

4

Malcolm brought his hand to her belly. It felt swollen, not flat like always, but bloated a tiny bit. A secret that only he could know. Angie usually had such firm abs. All that gymnastics and swimming. He loved to kiss her stomach softly, a feeling almost like love, or like the first light-headed buzz of drunkenness.

Giddy and high. Of all her body parts, he loved her belly best. Stupid as that sounded, since there were other outstanding parts to consider. But now this. Angela was full of some fluttering something in there, a ripening, a magical caterpillar.

Their baby butterfly.

What's in there? he wondered. *Does it look like me? Does it have my eyes? Does it even have eyes at all?* He realized, then, and once again for the millionth time that week, how little he knew about anything.

Stupid, he thought to himself.

Stupid fool.

5

He remembered an echo of a poem they taught in school. How there was a path in the woods—no, it was a fork, that was it—and a guy on a horse. This way? Or that way? That was the question. Who wrote that? Shakespeare? *Romeo and Juliet? What is that last line,* he wondered. Something about it making all the difference.

He told himself that he'd look it up someday, even as he knew that he never would. Who had time for it anyways. Or cared, actually?

It was easier to compare the pregnancy test to that scene in *The Matrix.* Here's a blue pill, here's a red pill. Neo had a choice. Go this way, or go that way? And that shit's going to make all the difference in the world. He played that scene out again in his mind: pee on that stick, baby, and let's cross our fingers for good luck.

Oh well.

No luck at all.

Now he was here. In this place.

Malcolm stretched out his legs, crossed at the ankles, tired of staring at the ceiling. It didn't feel right to watch videos on his phone. That would be crass, clueless. He wasn't a creep in a T-shirt. He flipped through the pages of a fitness magazine, *Healthy Living* or some shit. He sighed, yawned. A place like this, Planned Parenthood, the shit they do in here, a guy should be on his best behavior. Respectful. Sort of like in church. He took off his hat and placed it on the seat beside him. Groaned with boredom. And thought about that guy on the horse, Hamlet or something, wondering which path to cruise down.

"To be or not to be"! That was the quote!

Eenie, meenie, miney, moe.

Have a baby, or let it go.

6

It was supposed to bring them closer, in theory, but now a hazy distance grew between them. Ever since the pregnancy test, Angela had become super polite, killing him with cold kindness. "Yes, Malcolm." And "please" and "thank you" and "of course, you may." She said all the right words, but now the feeling was gone. No, it had morphed into something hard and implacable. Stone by stone, she built a wall between them. "Please" was one stone, "you're welcome" was another. And day by day, the wall grew higher.

All the while Malcolm thinking:

I don't see how this is all my fault.

7

I don't want you to come if you're just going to sit there playing games on your phone," Angela had said.

Malcolm couldn't imagine how it mattered what he did. But for once, wisely, he kept his big yap shut. After an appropriate pause, he said, "Jesus, Angie. I'm not going to play games while you're, you know . . ."

Privately, he wondered if there might be a television in the waiting room. Probably tuned to CNN or something serious like that. Fox Freaking News. Whatever. Maybe they'd let him change the channel. But of course he immediately saw how bad that would look. Him laughing at something on Comedy Central, while Angela was inside with Doctor Death.

Angela once saying to him:

I wonder if I'll go to hell for this?

8

B efore making the appointment, Angela had started reading about fetuses. That's how she typically dealt with stuff. That's what made her such a star in the classroom. She assembled the facts, studied everything, absorbed all the data. When does life begin? What is the right thing to do?

It was hard to say.

The whole world limping to extinction. But not today, not today.

It came down to this: 1) keep the baby and raise it, somehow; 2) adoption, give birth to the child and surrender it up to some perfect family, folks who could give it "a better life"; or 3) abortion, terminate the pregnancy, move on, try not to look back.

Like shutting off the lights. The flickering heartbeat, no more.

She x-ed out the computer window and closed her eyes for a moment. Angela loved the library, the cozy chairs, the books, the air-conditioning, and the hushed voices, overhearing people as they passed whispering about school or nail polish, the die-hard readers who arrived like methadone addicts strung out for the next bestseller. It inspired Angela, sitting there, taking it all in, even while wondering about this thing in her belly.

What to do, what to do?

9

She kissed Malcolm's neck, his face. "He'd be beautiful, you know."

"He?" Malcolm asked, tilting his head to better see Angela's face. *What mood is this?*

Her lips curled into a shy grin. "A boy, yes. That's how I think of him." Her hand moving automatically to her belly. "I know we can't keep him. But I just know he'd be beautiful."

"Yeah, if he looked like you," Malcolm said, kissing her. A part of his soul fluttered up from his heart and into her mouth, like a firefly.

10

Come fishing with me," he said.

"Seriously?"

"It's relaxing, you'll like it." He touched her hand, gently wrapped a finger around her pinky. "We'll lay out a blanket, bring something to eat. It'll be nice."

"Just us? Not the boys?"

Malcolm shrugged. She saw through him so easily. "I can't swear on my life about who is gonna be at the pond or not. I heard the guys were catching some decent-sized bass lately. If word gets around . . ."

"Go without me," Angela said.

He watched her, uncertain.

"It's okay, really," she assured him. "Go."

So he met up with the guys at the pond. They had a good time, laughed a lot, and everybody caught a fish. Except for Malcolm. "Damn. If I had any kind of luck at all, it would be bad," he complained.

Nothing felt right.

That day he almost threw his pole in the water and walked away.

Almost.

11

She had always imagined herself as a mother, for as long as she could remember. She pictured herself holding a small, fragile child—caring for it, loving it, being a great mom. And now she contemplated doing the exact opposite of that.

Malcolm watched her as she sat scowling on the grass, deep in thought. Finally, he told her, "I want to come."

"What?" Angela hadn't expected that. Hoped for it, yes, wished for it, wanted it. But she had been afraid to ask for it.

"I want to be there," he repeated.

"But you have to work."

He shook his head. "I'll quit if I have to, it's just Burger King. But I won't have to," he hurriedly added, seeing the look on her face. "I can get Fish to fill in for me."

"Fish?" she said. "That's his name?"

Malcolm laughed. A little flash of light darted between them, a dancing laser from retina to retina. "It's only Akeel, but we started calling him Fish a couple of weeks ago. He came in one day with a fishy smell and we've tagged him with it ever since."

Angela nodded, as if receiving important information. Her mind had traveled on to other things. "You can't tell anyone," she said.

"I won't," he promised.

"I'm serious, Mal. No one can ever, ever know about this."

He stepped forward, took her face in his hands—her smooth skin, those full lips—looked into her blazing gray eyes, and spoke in a slow, clear voice: "No one will know—and I'll be with you, every step of the way."

"Thanks," she said, almost smiling. A pause, followed by a question: "You hungry? Let's get a cookie at Marie's Bakery on Lark. One of those big, expensive black and whites. My treat."

12

And so the day came.

They took a bus into the city, turning what could have been a fifteen-minute drive into a fifty-minute adventure. The bus had been Angela's idea. Their secret journey. No one could ever know.

When they arrived, and Malcolm saw the dingy streets, he didn't want to get off. Some instinct told him to stay on, but Angela was already up and out the door. She moved purposefully, took long strides. He hurried to catch up with her on the sidewalk. According to the map on her phone, they had to walk a few blocks. To Malcolm, she had never looked more beautiful than in that moment. Chin up, determined. "Sketchy neighborhood," he observed.

Malcolm put his arm around Angie's shoulders, but instantly realized his mistake. She remained stiff, nothing soft in her body, which was moving like a bullet from a gun.

She had become steel.

He let his arm drop.

She surprised him when she said, "That's why they put these places here, you know, in the poor neighborhoods. The rich people don't want to see a Planned Parenthood near their pretty houses." She gestured to the sidewalk, the littered gutter, fast-food wrappers and rain-soaked cigarette butts and the colorful shimmer of oil stains on the pavement. "They don't want to know about what goes on in the real world."

Are you sure about this? he almost asked. But it was too late for that. They kept walking. She stopped when the Planned Parenthood building came into sight. Angela turned to him and said, "I don't regret having sex with you, Mal. And I'm glad it was you, I really am. I only regret being so stupid about it." She gave him a chaste kiss on his cheek, the way a mama might peck a little boy. She turned and started walking in the direction of a low, gray building. Malcolm followed.

Five people were gathered on the near corner across from the

building. They were holding signs. Three men, a woman, and—
they saw now, as they drew closer—a young girl who might have
been six years old. She held a sign that read, simply, *ABORTION
KILLS CHILDREN.*

Two middle-aged men leaned against a huge sign that was
nearly their size. It showed a huge photograph of a bloodied fetus
and read, *ABORTION at 21 WEEKS.* The woman, dressed all in
black, held a much smaller sign: *I Regret My Abortion.*

Hand on her elbow, Malcolm steered Angela across the street,
seeking a path where they could avoid the protesters. "Assholes,"
he muttered.

"It's what they believe," Angela said. "I guess they've got a
right."

"I guess," Malcolm answered, head fixed forward. "It sure feels
like we're being watched."

"And judged," Angela said.

He found her hand and squeezed it.

She squeezed back.

And that is how they arrived at the building, hand in hand. At
the last possible instant, she dropped his hand, pulled open the
door, and stepped into forever.

That's when he knew that she loved him, she truly did, but
she'd never forgive him for this.

13

"Angela?" A nurse appeared holding a clipboard, looking expectantly into the waiting room.

Angela rose too quickly, as if yanked by a puppeteer's string.

The nurse offered a tight smile, a nod, gestured with a hand. This way.

Her balance regained, Angela stepped forward. As an afterthought, she gave a quick, quizzical look back at Malcolm.

"Love you." The words stumbled from his throat. But if she heard, Angela didn't show it. She was on her own now. And so she walked through the door, down the hallway, and into another room. Simple as that.

Malcolm sat and stared at the empty space where, only moments before, his Angela had been.

14

He went to the desk and asked, "Um, do you have like some paper and a pen I could use?" And then, seeing the lady's face, added, "Please," an afterthought.

"We have scrap paper, is this all right?"

"Yeah, yeah, thanks."

He took it and went back to his crappy orange plastic chair.

And he started to write. The ideas came quickly, like music, like a river of words . . .

> I'm a quote collector, a garbage inspector, a hunter & a gatherer sifting through the trash of days, places, faces, looking for traces of meaning, seasons, reasons for being, treasons & betrayals, rights & wrongs & songs that last too long, girls in flight, sunlight & crazy caterpillars & buildings on fire, night mischief in the bushes, bodies that move & push & pull, the thoughts & feelings that move me, snag at my mind like thread from a sweater caught on a nail, unraveling, unreeling, recollecting, re-membering this right here, this right now, my girl in a faraway room, oh sweet angel, my Angela, scared & alone, a doctor in a white coat moving closer . . . what's that in his hand? WHAT'S THAT IN HIS HAND?!

Mal felt an acidic wave of sickness rush up his throat. He needed a drink of water real bad, right now. He stuffed the paper in his back pocket.

15

Malcolm got up to search for a water fountain. He returned to his seat, still feeling dry. Actually, it wasn't thirst at all, but boredom. He was so not a sitting-around kind of guy. His rest-less thoughts turned to his own father.

"He cut and run," Malcolm had once explained to Angela. They were alone in her house after school, both of her parents off at work, as usual. A sweet arrangement. "I hardly remember him anyway," he lied.

"Are you in touch with him? Where's he live?" she asked.

Malcolm looked away. A bitterness crept into his voice. "Don't know, don't care. Okay? He was never around for me anyway."

Angela listened, perfectly still.

"Last I heard," Malcolm continued, "he was down in Sarasota somewheres. Florida, some shit like that. He used to love the races. Horses, dogs, whatever. He gambled on the greyhounds."

"And he never calls you?" Angela asked.

A change came over him and Malcolm was done, locked up tight like those storefronts that bring down the iron gates with a clang at the end of day. He got up, opened the fridge in Angela's kitchen. Lifted out a beer. "You think your dad the detective would miss his own beer?"

Angela tilted her head in consideration. "How many has he got in there?"

Malcolm shifted things around, frowned. "I wouldn't call it a shit-ton."

Angela laughed. That boy could be cute sometimes. And he sure looked good shirtless. Those rope-like muscles. She felt something stir inside her. "We've got a second refrigerator in the basement. He usually keeps beer down there."

"Really?" Malcolm raised his eyebrows, catching something in her voice. "Let's go take a look-see."

"I don't know," she said, suddenly doubtful. She pictured the big brown couch in the basement, calculated the time before her folks would be home from work.

"Come on, darlin', let's go," Malcolm said, sweeping her up by the elbows. "It'll be fun."

"Yes," she agreed. "Let's."

16

R emembering something his father had once told him: "You've never been sailing, have you, Mal? Well, that's on me. Someday we'll rent a big sailboat and I'll show you the proper way to trim a jib."

That was his father all right: someday we'll do this, someday we'll do that. He talked the talk. Only thing was, someday had a way of never arriving. Tomorrow became today, and tomorrow was always the day after this one. Someday never came.

His father pointed ahead, twelve o'clock. "Listen up, Mal. Here's the deal with sailing. Let's say you and me want to head straight out, where the sun is rising on the horizon. Okay? In a sailboat, you can't never take the straight path!" He laughed with a hooting burst, further confusing his son. "You have to tack, you understand? You've got to *align with the wind*—you can't ignore the wind, you see, you've got to make it work for you. That means you've got to zigzag toward your goal, zigging left, zagging right, like a tailback avoiding tackles, left, then right, catching the wind in your sails and then, at just the precise moment, letting it go. You know what I'm saying, son? You've got to zigzag into the light."

Malcolm nodded to his father. "Yes, sir." But no, the boy didn't understand. *Zigzag into the light?* But now waiting in this sad room, Malcolm wondered if maybe he was headed to some obscure goal all along, just not in any direct way that normal people could figure out. That was sailing. That was life! Maybe that's what his father meant? There's water moving under you, tides and currents pulled by the moon, and a strong wind blowing all around your ears. So he zigged and zagged, wondering where this all might be taking him.

17

Waiting there, thinking it through, he scribbled a poem for Angela, top of his head.

THEN YOU APPEARED

It was like a spear
To my chest
Ribs cracking
Like the Grinch
That dude's heart exploding

The shock
The eruption I felt
And still feel . . .
Every day I fall in love

Still . . . and still
I'm falling

Then you appeared, then you appeared . . .

Before you I walked in a daze
In a maze,
Crazed
About nothing,
Going nowhere slow,
Bored bored bored

Then you appeared, then you appeared . . .

I wasn't unhappy
Wasn't happy neither
Just drifting
Aimless you know
A sail in any old wind
Cool breeze tangled up
In nowhere

Then you appeared, then you appeared . . .

Now we're here, you're in there
And I'm so sorry, girl
So sorry
That I've brought you

Such sadness
And I'm here to say
We will rise up
Together

Then you appeared, then you appeared . . .

I made myself a promise
A promise I will keep
I'll do better, angel,
I'll do better next time,
We can still make it
Together.
It's something worth
Fighting for, ain't it?
Ain't it something?

Staring at the tight scrawl on the page, Malcolm lost heart, no longer up for the task, not sure how to finish it. Endings didn't come easily.

18

Angela lay on a bed in a grim room. Pale green paint on the bare walls. Her feet in the stirrups. She heard a faint whir of machines. Beeps, signals, flashing lights. She was being monitored by computers. Heartbeat, pulse, things like that. She dared not look around.

She squeezed her eyes shut. Then opened them. Closed, then open, again and again, so it all felt like a flickering dream.

Angela thought, *This is where it will happen. The room I'll try to forget for the rest of my life. And now, now, now is when it will happen.*

And then it came, one final time, a warm hand on top of Angela's, and the question: "We are about to begin with the procedure. Are you absolutely sure this is what you want to do?"

Angela didn't answer, she couldn't answer. Instead, she was overwhelmed with feeling, saturated. The nurse waited. Angela acutely felt the weight of the hand upon her hand, saw the clear sympathetic gaze of the nurse's ice-blue eyes—she was still pretty, this much-older woman, handsome even, and by the ring on her finger, Angela was sure that she was married, perhaps with grown children of her own—and Angela knew for certain the answer.

What she must do.

Was she sure?

The words came to her lips.

Tears to her eyes.

The nurse nodded, her gaze steady and true. Then she handed Angela a box of tissues.

19

Malcolm imagined an inmate strapped to an electric chair, a jolt screaming through his body, and another jolt of the evil juice. Eyes rolling back in his head, pissing, shitting, convulsing in horror, dying.

Waiting, waiting, waiting. That was his job. To sit and wait for his girl. It was all he could do. A sensation of regret seeped from every portal, every nerve fiber. He was drowning in it.

My kid, he thought.

Malcolm wondered if maybe he should have said more, lobbied harder. *That's my child!* And he knew in that same instant how he didn't have the right stuff to be that baby's daddy. Oh, he'd love it, for sure. But he had no money, no real job, was still just a kid himself. Not a man.

He wanted to live.

If you have a baby, that makes you a man by definition. Some guys talked that way, like they believed it. Malcolm wasn't so sure about that. Anybody could make a baby. But what makes a man?

His phone vibrated. He'd been ignoring his texts and media accounts, Twitter, Instagram, the ceaseless digital feed. He unpocketed the phone to read a series of increasingly urgent texts:

"Hoops at the park, 2:00." And: "Where r u?" And: "Need your skills, brother! Be there."

He was missing the game. For a crazy instant, Malcolm calculated the math. If Angela got done soon, and he dropped her off fast—would she even be okay for that? He wasn't sure what condition she'd be in—he could still get to the park. Her house would be empty, both parents working, even on a Saturday. He could tuck her into bed, get her some water, a sandwich maybe, then head out for like two hours, tops, and still . . .

Selfish thinking, he knew it. There would be no b-ball today. Actually, no, there would be. The game would go on, with someone else taking his place.

Scrolling, he found an earlier text from Fish that he'd missed. Fish wrote apologizing, saying that he couldn't take Malcolm's morning shift at BK after all. Well, that sucked. Shit, shit, shit. Probably fired for that. The King don't go for no-shows. No, His Royal Highness, the King of Burgers, doesn't like that one bit.

Have it your way, my ass.

It was turning out to be one hell of a day.

20

He thought about his father. The man sure was on Malcolm's mind today. Guess it made sense. What with the baby—the procedure—and all.

There were memories, old photographs. A lot of it had been

scrubbed clean by his mother, empty pages in scrapbooks. The old man liked to drink, Malcolm remembered that much. Even from his youngest days, he remembered it.

"Hey, Mal, be a sport and get me a beer, will you?" his father had asked.

Young Malcolm used to love those assignments. An opportunity to win the approval from the lord of the manor.

Malcolm returned with the beer and waited, holding the cold glass bottle in his hands.

"Put it down right there. Thanks, Mal." Head inclined toward the racing form. His father loved following the horses—the old joke suddenly remembered—"With a shovel!" he used to say. You know, to pick up the manure on the street. Except in real life, that was the last thing his father would ever do. When things got messy, his father didn't pick up shit. He just cut and run, leaving Mom to deal with the mess (and the bills, and the kids).

Malcolm stood there in memory, just to the right of the chair, a boy waiting beside his father's elbow. The beer went to his father's lips. He tilted his head back, and back, squeezed his eyes shut from the cold pleasure of it. Malcolm watched in wonder as his father's Adam's apple bobbed up and down. Another long swig.

"Dad?"

"Yeah, Mal?" Not looking up.

"Want to go fishing tomorrow, maybe?" Malcolm asked.

"I do not," his father replied, laughing a little to himself.

Malcolm felt his heart drop like an autumn leaf—he could still remember that sinking, drifting feeling, the old man's easy rejection, even across ten years. Still remembering. Young Malcolm persisted. "Tommy caught a striper yesterday, a big one," he said.

The old man looked up. "A striper, huh?"

Malcolm nodded. "Yes, sir," he said, though he suddenly wasn't at all sure.

"We'll see, okay? Life's a little complicated these days."

"Thanks, Dad," Malcolm answered.

"Tell you what though," his father said. "I could sure use another cold one."

"Right away," Malcolm said, half skipping into the kitchen.

Turns out they did go fishing the next day, father and son with a cooler full of beer, sandwiches, and bait. Two thin lines going into the water, as nearly invisible as the memory itself. It was a happy day that Malcolm would never forget, no matter how hard he tried.

Inside a year, his father was gone for good, gone for bad, gone forever.

And now Malcolm turned his thoughts inward, as if gazing at his reflection in a mirror.

Is this it? he wondered. *Am I just like him? Worse, even? Not even man enough to bring my child into the world?* Malcolm grumbled out loud and then looked around, startled to find himself the object of inquisitive glances. He buried his face in a lousy magazine.

A nd then she appeared.

"How'd it go? Was it bad? Are you okay?"

A pause, a confusion. And a brand-new thought pushed its way into his mind.

Was it even possible?

"Did you go through with it?" he asked.

"Did you?"

Silence.

"Did you?"

She scarcely looked at him. Face ashen, eyes unfocused. Outside on the sidewalk, she saw the small crowd of protesters on the corner, still holding their horrible signs. She wouldn't avoid them this time. Angela lifted her chin, steadied herself, and moved forward, scared of nothing.

"Hey, wait up, I wrote you a poem," he called after her, remembering the folded paper in his pocket. "I wrote you a poem!"

*N*ot now, *Mal,* she thinks.

And Angela also thinks, as she moves past the street-corner protesters, *I am not ashamed of what I have done. I can look you in the eye, every one.*

She recalls all those Choose Your Own Adventure books she had loved as a child. So long ago. Those exciting choices upon which each story turned. "If you take the bus, turn to page 67. If you choose to wait, please turn to page 48." She loved flipping the pages back and forth, seeing how each new decision would bring about an entirely different turn of events.

Strange how those silly books were exactly like real life. Angela promises herself that she'll take a look at them again, those tattered books boxed away in a closet somewhere, along with her other childish things.

Choose your own adventure. Yes, yes. But she'd never imagined this awfulness. Angela now stepped into a story where there was no longer a fetus in her belly. Thrum, thrum, thrum. She walked to the rhythm of one heartbeat only, her heart, steady and firm, no longer followed by the tiny echo of a second one. The baby that would not be; please turn to page 63.

Sweet Mal still tugging at her sleeve, asking questions, chattering on about some poem he's just written. She thinks, *Oh Mal, can't you see? I am the poem.*

I am strong, and brave, and beautiful. And though my bones feel heavy, and my heart aches, I will be the one who writes the next verse.

I am the one who decides.

Angela smiles softly, lost in thought, takes Mal's hand, and crosses the street.

THE GOOD BROTHER
Patrick Flores-Scott

The bell rings. I race out of geometry. Scribble my signature on the dismissal sheet at the front office. Run down the streets of Burlington.

I have to get home to meet Javier. I can't be late to the hearing that might change my life forever.

Thoughts bounce around my head at warp speed till I grab a hold of one and can't let go.

Four days.

Four days.

Just four little days.

Four days is ninety-six hours.

Three days less than a week.

Something between one-seventh and one-eighth of a month.

There are four-day weekends.

In four short nights the Mariners played a four-game series against the Angels.

In four days Javier could fall in and out of love . . . and fall in love again.

I don't slow down as I make the turn onto tree-lined Salmon Street. I picture myself back in immigration jail, listening to Ms. Hernandez. I hear her lawyer voice in my brain. *José, you crossed four days too late to be eligible for Deferred Action for Childhood Arrivals.*

What does that mean?

It means if your dad had crossed you over the border four days earlier, you wouldn't be in this jail. Children whose parents brought them over before the DACA cutoff date can apply to stay in the country without threat of deportation. You only missed the cutoff date by four days. You were so close that we're going to ask the judge for special consideration. Don't get your hopes up too high but I think we've got a good chance.

Ms. Hernandez is my lawyer because she's my mom's best friend's sister. She and mamá met a long time ago and now Ms. Hernandez is like family. And she's the best immigration lawyer in Western Washington, so I believe her when she says we've got a good chance.

I get to the apartment. The front door is locked. I knock fast.

No one answers.

"Javier, open up!"

Nothing.

I dig out my key and wrestle with the lock till the door springs open. "Javi, you in here?"

No answer. *Where the hell are you, brother? We have to be in Seattle in an hour and a half. This is my life you're messing with.*

Maybe I got the time wrong. I recheck the text from Javi.

Ms H called hearing changed to afternoon @4
meet u @ home by 2

It's already past two. Where are you, Javi?

Brother or no brother, I have to get dressed and get out of here. If I'm late, they'll deport me for sure.

I go to my room and open my dresser. Reach for my lucky polo.

But there are no shirts in my shirts drawer.

What the hell?

I pull open each drawer, top to bottom.

Nothing. All my clothes are gone.

I go to Javi's dresser.

His clothes are all there.

Fucking Javi and his pranks!

I don't have a choice. I have to find something decent in his pile of black thrift-shop rebel clothes. There's one button-down shirt. A pair of jeans with only one hole. Some shiny shoes.

I look in the mirror and I'm him.

I'm Javi.

Shit.

I'm about to leave when I see a fat, white envelope on my bed.

I reach down. Pick it up. Slide my fingers inside and pull out a stapled pile of papers. I drop the envelope and start reading. It's a letter. A letter from Javi.

I read every word.

Oh no.

Oh my God.

My empty dresser was no joke.

I roll up the letter and fly out the door.

What has Javi done?

One bus ride through the tulip fields, over the river, into Mount

Vernon. I sprint two blocks to the office and push through the front door. The bell jingles and Ms. Hernandez looks up from behind her desk. "Where the hell have you been, Javier?"

I try to answer the question but she just goes on and on, bawling me out for missing my brother's hearing. Stuff about how he needed my support and how I could have made a difference.

I finally just interrupt and tell her Javi lied to me. "He texted me the time got switched. He stole my clothes. It was Javi at the hearing. It was Javi dressed up like me."

Ms. Hernandez springs to her feet and locks the office door. She gets in my face. Looks me right in the eye. "Oh my God. You're—"

"I'm José."

"Oh my God. Oh my God." She puts her hands on her head and walks back behind her desk. Drops into her chair. Points a finger at me. "You are here. And your brother is on a one-way flight to Mexico. Oh my God, why? Why did Javier—"

I tell Ms. Hernandez I don't have a clue why he did it. But that's a lie. The letter is right there, folded inside my pocket. I know I have to give it to her. But I can't do it. I'm not ready for what comes after.

So I ask her about the hearing. "What did he say?"

"Javier?"

"No. The judge."

"José, he agreed you were a model member of the community. But he maintained that the DACA cutoff date was not arbitrary and cruel. So he denied the appeal. That was that."

"I can't believe it, Ms. Hernandez. I didn't think there was a chance we'd lose."

"Seriously, José? We went over the possibility a hundred times."

"I know. But there was a part of me that believed . . . because ever since we came here, I've never messed up. I've done everything right."

"Oh, José . . ." She says it like I'm a five-year-old. "Sometimes it just doesn't matter."

I sink into the chair and close my eyes. I imagine mamá and papi at the hearing—even though I know there's no way they could risk going. I picture them sobbing uncontrollably, heartbroken as the judge announces his decision.

I ask Ms. Hernandez if she called them.

"Yes. They were devastated, of course. Have they seen you yet? Do they know about Javier?"

"No. And I don't know how to tell them. I don't know what to do. I need you, Ms. Hernandez." I pull out the letter. Unfold the pages. Slide them across the desk. "You have to read this. You have to help me."

Dear Jos,

Surprise, dude. Your hearing was this morning. And if you haven't seen me by now, it means you been deported and I took your place. I'm the one headed to live with Tía Rosario, an aunt I never met, in a town I never been to. It means I'm figuring out how to make my way with no friends, no goals, and shitty-ass pocho Spanglish. Don't worry about me though, brother. I'm a survivor. I'm gonna make it down there and give you a chance to reach your dreams in the good ol' US of A.

Man, we had some good times, Jos. We fooled so many people. It was a rush every time. I know that's why you kept your hair long and curly, just like mine. So we could switch whenever we wanted.

Admit it, you like playing the bad-boy role every now and then. Being me. Taking my tests. Running with my crazy friends for a few hours. Ever since kindergarten, we been fooling teachers. Our friends. Even mamá and papi. We're more identical than identical.

But that's all on the outside, huh, bro?

Okay, right about now, you're asking yourself, *Why did Javi do this for me?*

Good question.

You remember Juárez, Jos? When we were little kids waiting to cross the border? Mamá was going to take one of us first? Then papi was gonna cross over a few days later with the other? You were always gonna go over first. No questions. You remember that?

Jos, I really, really wanted to go first.

You're older than me by ten minutes. You always been first at everything. You always been better than me. Smarter than me. I wanted to feel how you feel.

I talked mamá and papi into it and I got over the border and we stayed at Ricky's place in El Paso. You came over a few days later and by then I was already king of the apartment complex. I chose my side of the bed first. I knew where everything was. I already had a bunch of friends. I could teach you everything because I knew stuff and you didn't. So, for a little while, I was smarter than you.

Then we headed up to Washington and you turned into the smart, good, first brother again.

Anyways, me coming over first is why you spent two weeks in immigration jail, while I walked around free, feeling like an asshole.

It should have been me in there, Jos.

That's not the only reason I took the fall for you. Jos, you think you're smart. Everyone thinks you're smart. But the truth is, you're the stupidest smart person I ever met and I don't think you could survive one week in Mexico. You bought into all the *dream-big-and-work-hard-and-you-will-succeed* crap and you got soft. Maybe you were just born soft, I don't know. Whatever it is, Mexico would chew you up and spit you out, brother.

When we walked out of that 7-Eleven, you were going on and on about your future. Being junior class president. Killing your SATs. Flying off to some fairyland college with Elena.

All I could think was, *You ain't got no papers, dumbass.*

And I know you were thinking, *I got the best grades in my class and I play football and volunteer at one animal shelter and one people shelter. I'm so perfect and I work so hard, colleges gonna hook me up regardless of my status.*

Then, right on cue, Border Patrol walks our way. I was practically shitting my pants, Jos. Everybody up here knows la migra ain't shaking down no Canadians. But you were all calm and cool, thinking we didn't do anything wrong, so we got no problem.

Even after they arrested us, and even after they left you in jail and let me go, you kept on believing. *They're gonna let me out of here, Javi. I never been in any kind of trouble. There's no way they'll deport me.*

You got blinders on, Jos.

I know that's what it takes to succeed in this country. Narrow your vision so you don't see the shitty mess this place is. So you can believe in right and wrong . . . good and bad. *Justice.* And you can chase the fantasy. I'm sure that can actually work, Jos . . . if you got papers and parents who got papers.

But that don't work for us. So, unlike you, Jos, I got my eyes wide open. And what do I see?

I see R-E-A-L-I-T-Y.

Yeah, there is good in the world. There are good people and you're one of them. But the REALITY is, there are a whole lot of other people who don't give a shit about you. And those are the people that make the rules. They make the rules so that they win. And so that we lose. And that's the truth, brother.

Yeah, for now it's true what Ms. Hernandez says. You heard her. As long as you keep my name outta trouble, you'll be safe from deportation with the DACA. So go ahead, Jos, keep doing the All-American boy act and keep up all your hoping. But you gotta be honest with yourself. You know DACA don't include no green card and no path to citizenship. And you know it ain't even a law, so judges can do whatever they want and the next prez can scribble his pen and make it go away. Then that tiny bit of hope you got? It's nothing. So unless a bunch of fat old white pendejos miraculously turn into sensible caring people and change a bunch of stupid laws, that's the reality you're stuck with.

In the meantime, it's up to you to pull off the biggest switch we ever tried. I know you're gonna want to charge ahead and transform me into a success story real fast. But, Jos, if you do that, people will notice. They will ask questions. You'll be risking everything. So you have to be patient. You have to go real slow. There's time to turn this into a loser-makes-good story. But for now, you're just a loser. Don't forget that.

You can do it, man. But check it out, the following is background info on what's going on with me right now. Pay attention. Read closely. This is all extremely important:

I got detention for skipping Olson's class. You should probably show up for that. I'm pretty much failing chemistry and math. And my LA teacher, Mrs. Donaldson, hates me, so watch out. Oh, and PE, too. Don't ever suit up for PE this year. People will definitely suspect something. I'm thinking you should probably just fail three out of four of those classes this semester. After that you can turn up the smart one class at a time, real gradual, until I'm straight A's. That'll be nuts, man. All those lame-ass teachers will get all weepy and say, *Young man came from nothing. He even lost his beautiful perfect twin brother, but somehow, he's risen above the pain and suffering to reach his true potential. Javier Mendoza is an inspiration to us all.*

Colleges love that kind of shit. So if the DREAM Act passes someday you can take my name to college for real. Won't that be something? (***WARNING! Due to risk of injury or death, DO NOT HOLD BREATH while waiting for fat old white pendejos to do the right thing.***)

This one's gonna be real hard, Jos. But for you to even have a chance at your dreams, you have to make sacrifices. You cannot keep it going with Elena. You cannot even tell Elena that you're me. If you do, you know she'll tell one of her gossipy friends and that friend will spread the chisme and some jealous girl gonna Facebook it and you'll end up down at Tía Rosario's with me.

I know it sucks. You and Elena been together forever. She's a great girl. Great family. Real pretty. On her way to some primo college. Some great job. I know you two already been talking about marriage someday, traveling the world, getting old and wrinkly together. Get real, Jos! You're sixteen and you got no papers. Sure, she loves you for now. But down the road when this stuff really matters? You think she's gonna stick by you? Plenty of legal fish in the sea, Jos. All I'm sayin'.

So let Elena think I'm still me. Give her your address in Mexico and I'll write her a beautiful little letter telling her I love her but it's over between us. Long-distance relationships and all that mierda. Don't worry, I'll be sweet like you. Throw in some poetry. Let her down easy as possible.

Oh, and watch out for Susi. She'll be looking for you in the halls. She will probably most definitely want to slap your face for me cheating on her with Alexis. You know Alexis? The one with the gangland brother who picks her up after school sometimes? Got all those tattoos wrapped around his neck. He runs with Southside Vernon 13 gang, Jos. That guy is scary as shit.

Alexis will wanna slap you, too. She is full-on pissed at me, so try to stay out of her way. She's all convinced I got her pregnant even though we just messed around a little tiny bit one time. It's pretty much almost biologically impossible, Jos, so you got my word. IT AIN'T MINE.

Your buddies, Jos. You gotta stay away from Carlos and Freddy for a few months or everyone's gonna wonder why I'm all of a sudden hanging out with nerds. And you know you gotta be tight with the three amigos, Walter, Ronnie, and Momo. I know you think they're asshole losers. And you're probably right. But they got my back. You're gonna need those guys.

They know all the shit that's going on with me right now. They know about Alexis's brother and how he got me messed up in some stuff I didn't know how to say no to. Please do not hate me. Dude cornered me. He said he'd call Border Patrol on mamá and papi. I couldn't get out of it. I'm so sorry. It kills me to even tell you about this, but I got no choice. And neither do you. It's Southside Vernon 13 business, Jos. One hundred percent serious shit.

So the deal is, there's a big plastic bag under my bed. You gotta take that to an address that's on a tiny light-blue Post-it note in my wallet. (*Your* wallet. I switched all our stuff this morning. And you're gonna need my phone. It's in my socks drawer.) And you're gonna do this tonight, Jos. Tonight at 11:30. Oh, and don't get that light-blue Post-it confused with the dark-blue Post-it. The dark-blue Post-it is where you wanna take the stuff that the guys at the light-blue Post-it address are gonna give you in exchange for the contents of that plastic bag under my bed. Anyways, when you drop that stuff off at the end of the night (12:00. Be on time!), I really think you should just tell Lazy Eye—that's Alexis's brother—and those other SV13 guys that you admire them and their work, and you've enjoyed your time with them, but that you respectfully decline their invitation to be a regular member of their organization. Maybe tell them papi has cancer and you gotta be with him all the time? Or mamá? Yeah, better if mamá has the cancer.

And you might wanna have the gun when you tell them that. The gun is in the back of my shirts drawer wrapped in my Metallica tee. Actually, you might *not* wanna take the gun. On the other hand, you could take the gun and unload the bullets right in front of them and hand it over? And maybe cry? Or just run? I dunno. You could go in there with it loaded, waving it around, shouting like an unpredictable lunatic? It's up to you. Feel it out. I trust that you'll make the right decision.

If you do choose to take the gun loaded—this is really

important, Jos—YouTube some videos so you know what the hell you're doing. Search the key words "loading and firing a semiautomatic Smithfield LX10" and "gun safety."

I promise you the gun was not my idea. Lazy Eye gave it to me. He thought I should maybe definitely have some protection for when I got to the light-blue Post-it. So yeah, it might be a good idea to have it on you. But again, totally your call. Do what feels right.

Anyhow, talk to the tres amigos about all this. Their numbers are in my cell. They're planning on backing me up. And Momo thought it would be a good idea for his cousin, Fabio, to shadow me tonight. Fabio is in a different gang, so if shit gets out of hand, he'll know how to handle it. He's a little crazy, too, which I think totally works in your favor. Do not mention any of this to Lazy Eye.

So the messed-up thing about this whole situation is that because of me fooling around with Alexis, Lazy Eye knows where we live. He's been to the apartment, Jos. So you really gotta do this thing. Just get over this one little hurdle for yourself. And for mamá and papi so those guys don't come around anymore.

Jos, I know I seem pretty cool all the time. But the truth is, a lot of shit seems to be finding me. You been so busy and mamá and papi are always working. I been able to hide some stuff from you. Like I been getting nervous a lot. And even scared. I just feel like shaky all the time. About everything. Like I can't even barely hold my shit together anymore.

That's not really why I decided to become you. Okay, I'm sure it has something to do with it, but mostly it's because I really believe you got a chance in the US. If stuff breaks your way, you got a shot at a great future.

I don't.

Actually, maybe thanks to you, I do. Who knows? Maybe someday I'll be able to come back. And you can go be you again. And I can go back to being me with this amazing new successful life you created for me.

Don't worry, though. I'm not holding my breath. I got my ojos wide open. No blinders here. I know this whole deportation is just gonna mean more struggle for all of us. But I'll let a little piece of me hope for the best. I learned that from you, brother. I know I give you a hard time about being perfect and innocent and all that, but you taught me how to hope. You taught me what it means to be good.

And I'm going to give it a try. This is just the first step for me. I swear I'm gonna make it work. I'm gonna make Mexico work. And maybe, just maybe . . .

All my love to you, brother.

All my love to mamá and papi.

Abrazos a todos,

Javier

Ms. Hernandez looks up from the letter.

All she can say is "Oh my God" a bunch more times.

"What do I do, Ms. Hernandez?"

"I don't know."

"You gotta have some idea."

"Here's what you don't do: you do not go anywhere near that deal, José. You hear me? You do not go anywhere near any SV13. You do not touch that gun. You stay away from that Fabio guy and your lunatic brother's friends. Got it?"

"But, Ms. Hernandez—"

"You get messed up in all that and there's only one way this story ends. I've seen it too many times." She leans in and looks me square in the eye. "I lost my little brother to guys like that."

She lets that idea hang there for a minute.

"I can't bear the thought of them getting you, too. I'd never be able to look your mom in the eye again."

"I'm sorry about your brother, Ms. Hernandez, but if I don't do that deal, I'm dead faster."

She looks down at the ground. She knows I'm right.

"You think I should call the police, don't you?"

"Yes, José. I do."

"Ms. Hernandez, if I don't show up, and the cops do, Lazy Eye will know I ratted them out. And he knows where we live."

She looks down at the desk. Then back at me. She sees my face and immediately looks away again. "I'm so sorry about all of this, José."

"That's it?"

She doesn't say anything.

"I'm sorry, too, Ms. H."

I snatch Javier's letter off her desk, turn my back to Ms. Hernandez, and head for the door. But before I get there, she's got a grip on my shoulder.

"Stop, José."

I turn to her.

"You have to leave here."

"That's what I'm trying to do."

"Listen to me: you have to leave this city. This state."

"But my parents—"

"SV13 will be looking for you. You need a new name. A new identity."

"I got a new identity."

"Wrong one. Look, stay here tonight and we can go back to court tomorrow. We'll sneak you in there and tell the judge the truth about what Javier did and see if we can get you deported."

"On purpose?"

"It's the safest way."

"I can't leave my parents alone, Ms. Hernandez."

"Your parents have to leave here, too. For their own safety."

"Our whole life is here."

"Your life?" She gives me the sad-little-kid look again. "You're not in control of that, José."

"I can't just leave, Ms. Hernandez. I have to do the right thing."

"José, sometimes the right thing means you just do the best you can under rotten circumstances."

"I can do better than that."

"Someday. Hopefully. But for now . . ."

"For now?"

"I'm going to get you out of here. I have a cousin in a small town outside Boise. I don't condone this, but he sets people up with temporary documents. Until they get settled. He owes me a couple favors. You could stay at his place till you and your parents get back on your feet. There's work picking onions."

"What the hell, Ms. Hernandez?"

"Are your parents at work?"

"Yeah."

"At Barringer's?"

"Yes."

"Get them on the phone."

"*Ms. Hernandez . . .*"

"Now."

My mom picks up after one ring. Ms. Hernandez takes my phone. Tells her there's an emergency and she's coming to pick them up.

She hands me the phone back. She closes the blinds and says, "Stay put till we get back. Nobody can know where you are."

"Is this for real?"

"SV13 is for real."

"I gotta call Elena."

"José, I need to borrow your phone again."

I hand it over.

She drops it and puts the heel of her lawyer shoe right through it.

"What the hell?"

"I'm sorry, but no one can know anything. No one can know you're here."

She reaches for her office phone and disconnects the receiver. Puts it in her purse so I can't make any calls. She pulls out her keys and makes her way to the door. "We'll grab some clothes at the apartment fast and be back for you as soon as we can. We can make it to Boise before morning."

She slams the door behind her, then immediately opens it and pops her head back in. "A client left a razor in the bathroom cabinet. There's scissors and a mirror in my desk. Lose the curls. Lose all of it. No one can see you looking like your brother. Or like you."

The door slams again before I can get a word out.

I walk to the window and lift up a corner of the blinds. I watch Ms. Hernandez close her car door. Her tires squeal as she backs out and speeds away.

I stand there, paralyzed, as it all sinks in. *We're moving to Idaho. We're leaving Burlington.* And it's for the best. Because Ms. Hernandez is keeping us safe. She'll be back with mamá and papi soon to take us away. Ms. Hernandez is just doing the right thing.

Now I have to do the right thing.

I rifle through the desk drawer and find the mirror and scissors. I head to the bathroom and stand at the sink. My long curls pile up on the floor until there's nothing left to cut. I soap my messed-up head and shave the rest off. Real slow. I pick the curls up off the floor. Throw them in the toilet and flush them down. I run my palm over my naked head and look in the mirror.

I'm not Javier anymore.

I'm not me anymore.

I take a seat and lay my head on the desk. I close my eyes and try to clear my mind as I wait for my next new life to begin.

Then I look at the door.

And I can't stop the thoughts this time . . . *I didn't choose to be born into this life. I didn't choose to cross over. I didn't choose when to cross over. I didn't choose to move to this town. I didn't choose to miss my hearing. I didn't choose my brother's life. I didn't choose to move to Idaho. I didn't choose to be stuck in this office. I didn't choose to be stuck.*

I didn't choose to be stuck.

Ms. Hernandez isn't stuck. She just opened that door and walked right through like it was no big deal. Like she could walk out whatever door she wants. Come and go whenever she wants.

I got a right to not be stuck.

My parents always tell us they came here—and they work so hard—so me and Javier could have a better life.

I got a right to that life.

I think about Carlos and Freddy. All the stuff we've done together. How they helped me get to where I am. All the plans we made. I can't imagine leaving them. And Elena. She's everything. I love her as much as anybody ever loved another person. I can't imagine living my life without her.

I reach down and feel Javier's phone in my pocket. I pull it out and check the time. Ms. Hernandez and my parents won't be back here for at least ten minutes.

I roll the chair over and pull up a corner of the blinds again.

I see the world outside this office. I see the new me reflected in the glass. Staring back. Waiting for me to say something. Waiting for me to do something.

So I do.

I start making my own choices.

I choose to stand. I choose to pull up all the blinds. I choose to walk right up to that door. I choose to reach out my hand. I choose to grab the handle. I choose to turn the handle.

I choose to push the door open.

And I choose to walk through it.

About the Authors

JAY CLARK is the author of *Finding Mr. Brightside*, which author Jerry Spinelli (*Stargirl*) calls "one of my favorite YA books ever," and *The Edumacation of Jay Baker*, which *Booklist* praised in a starred review: "The magic lies in the telling." He's also a random blogger. Surprisingly popular entries like "How to Stop Hating People in 15 Minutes" and "8 Tips for Posting Your Best Selfie Yet!" can be found on his website at jayclarkbooks.com. He lives in Columbus, Ohio.

KRISTIN ELIZABETH CLARK lives and writes in northern California, where she has worked as a child advocate within the juvenile justice system, and as a children's theater producer. Her first young adult novel, *Freakboy*, received three starred reviews, was on the ALA Rainbow Project Top Ten Best Fiction for Young Adults reading list, and was a Bank Street College Best Book of the Year. She is currently at work on a second novel for young adults. Visit her online at kristinelizabethclark.com.

HEATHER DEMETRIOS is the author of several novels, including the critically acclaimed *Something Real*, which won the Susan P. Bloom

Children's Book Discovery Award; its multi-platform companion, *The Lexie Project*; and *I'll Meet You There*. She has an MFA from Vermont College of Fine Arts and is the founder of Live Your What, a project dedicated to creating writing opportunities for underserved youth. She is currently developing a novel based on her short story. Visit her online at heatherdemetrios.com.

STEPHEN EMOND is the creator of the *Emo Boy* comic series; two illustrated young adult novels, *Happyface* and *Winter Town*; *Steverino*, a comic strip that ran in his local newspaper in Connecticut; and, most recently, *Bright Lights, Dark Nights*. He can be found at his website, stephenemond.com.

PATRICK FLORES-SCOTT was a longtime public school teacher in Seattle, Washington, before becoming a stay-at-home dad and early-morning writer in Ann Arbor, Michigan. Patrick's first novel, *Jumped In*, was a YALSA Best Fiction for Young Adults title, an Amelia Elizabeth Walden Award Finalist, an NCSS-CBC Notable Book for Social Studies, and a Bank Street College Best Book of the Year. Visit him online at patrickfloresscott.com.

FAITH ERIN HICKS is a writer and artist living in Halifax, Nova Scotia. Her previous works include *Zombies Calling, The War at Ellsmere, Brain Camp* (with Susan Kim and Laurence Klavan), *Friends with Boys, Nothing Can Possibly Go Wrong* (with Prudence Shen), the Bigfoot Boy series (with J. Torres), *The Last of Us: American Dreams* (with Neil Druckmann), and the Eisner Award–winning *The Adventures of Superhero Girl*. Learn more about Faith on her website at faitherinhicks.com.

TRISHA LEAVER is the author of *The Secrets We Keep*, which *VOYA* hailed as a "brilliant novel." She has also co-written the novels *Creed, Sweet Madness,* and *Hardwired.* Trisha lives on Cape Cod, Massachusetts, with her husband and children. Visit her website at trishaleaver.com.

KEKLA MAGOON is the author of several books for children and young adults, including *How It Went Down*, a Coretta Scott King Honor Book; *37 Things I Love*; *X* (with Ilyasah Shabazz); and *The Rock and the River,* winner of the John Steptoe New Talent Award. She is a Vermont-based writer, editor, speaker, and educator. Learn more about Kekla on her website, keklamagoon .com.

MARCELLA PIXLEY is a middle-school language arts teacher and a writer. Her poetry has been published in various literary journals, and she has been nominated for a Pushcart Prize. She is the author of *Without Tess* and *Freak,* which received four starred reviews and was named a *Kirkus Reviews* Best Book of the Year. She lives in Westford, Massachusetts, with her husband and two sons. Visit her on the Web at marcellapixley.com.

JAMES PRELLER's first novel for young adults, *Before You Go,* was praised by the *New York Times Book Review* as a book that "makes us care about [the characters] . . . and wonder about them when they're gone." He is also the author of several novels for younger readers, including *Six Innings; Bystander,* the recipient of numerous state reading awards; and *The Fall.* He lives with his family in Delmar, New York. Visit him at jamespreller.com.

JASON SCHMIDT was born in Oregon in 1972. In his debut young-adult memoir, A *List of Things That Didn't Kill Me,* he tells the story of growing up with an abusive father, who contracted HIV and ultimately died of AIDS when Jason was a teenager. Jason has a law degree and lives with his family in Seattle, Washington.

JORDAN SONNENBLICK's young adult titles include *Are You Experienced?; Drums, Girls, and Dangerous Pie; Notes from the Midnight Driver;* and *After Ever After,* all of which were published to great acclaim. He is also the author of the Dodger and Me series for younger readers. A former middle-school English teacher, he lives with his family in Bethlehem, Pennsylvania. Visit him online at jordansonnenblick.com.

Jacket Photography Credits

REALITY

**REAL BOOKS FOR
REAL TEENS**

To discover more authors and stories like those found in this anthology—as well as behind-the-scenes content, exclusive author bonus material, and downloadable reading guides—visit ReaLITyReads.com.

REALITYREADS.COM

FARRAR STRAUS GIROUX   FEIWEL AND FRIENDS   HENRY HOLT   IMPRINT   ROARING BROOK PRESS   SQUARE FISH   FIRST SECOND

IMPRINTS OF MACMILLAN CHILDREN'S PUBLISHING GROUP